The Maid
of the Mist

The Maid of the Mist

Melissa Franckowiak

ISBN 13: 978-1-7326808-1-4
Library of Congress Control Number: 2018902021
MelissaCrickard, Grand Island, NY

CHAPTER 1

M any Indian legends have been told about the mighty Niagara River, but none as mysterious as the tale of the young Indian princess, Lelewala, who went over the great Niagara Falls in her canoe. Lelewala was quite a storyteller herself, and so it seemed only fitting that she was destined to live out a magnificent story of her own, that would be passed on through the generations of Indian tribes inhabiting the Niagara Peninsula. Of course, there are different versions of the story, and the most memorable of the fables is the one told by Lelewala herself, but I'm afraid that many generations have passed since Lelewala left this world, so you'll have to listen to mine.

Now back when Lelewala was just a girl, in the early 1700's, the river wasn't yet known as the Niagara. The name of the fierce river was borrowed from the name of Lelewala's tribe, the Onguiaahra, or neutral, tribe.

It kind of sounds like Niagara, though, doesn't it?

The Onguiaahra tribe was a peace loving tribe, and Lelewala's father, the great Chief Honovi, led a tribe of skilled hunters. Deer populated the land now known as Goat Island, and every harvest back then was a plentiful one, abundant with fields of golden corn and squash. It was a beautiful time for the Onguiaahra, and Lelewala knew, even when she was very young, that she had a gift for storytelling. She probably got her talent from her mother, Eyota, but it's hard to tell.

One evening in the Indian village, when Lelewala was no more than five years old or so, she gathered around the fire with the other children, including her older brother, Dyani, and his friend, Inola. Inola was destined to be a great hunter—The Great Spirit had willed it. The tribal council was gathered in the longhouse on this night, but Eyota, Lelewala's mother, came out every now and then to quiet the children.

But it was hard for Lelewala to keep quiet.

Her heart was filled with a passion. She had stories to tell, an excitement she couldn't hold in a moment longer, and her soul bubbled with a livelihood that she wanted to share with the whole tribe. This evening, she was chasing Dyani around the fire, pretending she was a fierce water serpent. The younger children screamed with delight. The teenagers practiced their war calls and hooted and hollered until Eyota, for the third time, came out to hush them. When they were quietly seated on the ground under the stars, one of the youngest girls spoke.

"Tell us a story, Lelewala," the young girl, Anasi, said. Anasi was no more than three or four. "Tell us. Tell us."

Lelewala thought for a moment, then she started. "Once there was a great naked bear."

"*Ewwww*," shrieked the child. "Gross."

"Did the bear smell bad?" asked a boy.

Lelewala smiled. She brushed her dark hair from her shoulders and she fixed the feather in her headdress and she waited until everyone was quiet. Then she continued. "Naked bear was a monstrous, man-eating creature with no fur and a huge head."

Dyani wrinkled his nose and sat beside his sister. He was skeptical. "Why did all his fur fall out?"

"Because he ate little boys and girls," Lelewala yelled.

"*Ahhhhh!* This is too scary." The little girl hid behind a log, peering out periodically.

Inola leaned in closer. Even as a young boy, the tribe knew Inola would hunt great beasts and feed the entire tribe. There was a certain fire, a determination, in his dark eyes. "Yeah, but there's got to be a way to kill the bear. A great hunter would know what to do."

Lelewala smiled sweetly at him. "Naked bears are nearly impossible to kill, but they can be defeated by shooting arrows into their feet. And they can only chase a hunter who has not yet found its trail."

"Whoa," said the little boy seated beside Inola.

"What do you mean?" Inola asked.

"Once you find the trail of the Nyagwaheh bear, he must run from you," she shouted.

Just then, a group of older boys sneaked up and ran out from behind the longhouses, dressed in bear costumes and yelping war cries, circling the children. The young boys and girls shrieked, and they ran around in circles and they covered their ears. Lelewala winked at Inola, and she nodded and she giggled.

"*Arrrghhh,*" cried Anasi.

"Children!" her mother pulled back the deer skin tarp and peeked out of the entrance.

"Lele, your stories are the best," said Dyani. "One day, I'm going to be the best hunter in all The Land, and I'm going to slay the Nyagwaheh."

"Ah, there's no such thing as a giant naked bear," said Erami, an older boy.

"Phew," said the little girl, who passed out on her mat of corn husks, hysterical. She covered her forehead. Her feet fell down together as she lay on her back.

"Sorry, mama," she called.

Dyani aimed his bow and arrow at the oak tree beside them and he drew back and he released the arrow and he missed. He grimaced. Eyota came out of the longhouse and approached the children and placed her hand on Lelewala's shoulder.

After the teenage boys dispersed, she said to Dyani, "There are many truths in your sister's words."

"How does she know all this stuff?" Dyani frowned. "She's just a kid."

Eyota smiled at Lelewala, who was quiet, and she looked at Dyani. "She listens patiently. She observes. She has a gift."

"Lele's stories sound so real," Dyani said.

Her mother pointed to the starry sky. The autumn air crisp and dry raised the hairs on her neck, and Lelewala could see her breath now.

Eyota said, "Look to the sky. The great hunter slain the bear and ate it."

Her mother pointed to the constellation of stars that looked like a big pot with a curved handle. The moon was bright, and there wasn't a cloud in the sky now. The smell of the rushing waters and the dew on the crops reached them. Lelewala laid down on her mat beneath the stars. Dyani followed.

"Now look around you at the forest, children," said her mother. "The bear's blood falls from the heavens and colors the leaves of the maple trees scarlet."

"In autumn," she said, excitedly. "My favorite time."

"Yes, but the hunters are no longer in the mountains. The naked bear carried them up to the sky. The bear came back to life. As the moons pass, each year, and the sky moves once more towards spring, the bear slowly rises to his feet and begins the chase again. See..." Then where her mother lay gazing up at the sky, she pointed up to the heavens. The bear and the hunters seemed to come to life above them, even as Lelewala closed her eyes and fell into a brisk dream.

CHAPTER 2

The bountiful seasons changed, and five years later, the Onguiaahra tribe remained peacefully along the Niagara, thriving, growing in population. Never once had they gone hungry during the cold winters. The region radiated an energy unmatched, as it does today, with the soil giving back more each year, dispersing its yields among the faithful farmers. The fields scattered across them the alpha and the omega of the Indians' history, with a zest that Lelewala could breathe, but not see. Both channels of the river came alive that year with walleye and leaping Coho salmon and brown trout.

Each day, the young hunters brought back deer and turkey and sometimes, a moose, whose meat was exquisite. The harvests were kind to the Onguiaahra. The women picked the corn and beans and squash. The Indian children helped in the village, preparing meals and looking after the smaller children and gathering firewood.

The land surrounding the Onguiaahras' home was not always so peaceful, however, and one day in autumn, when a war broke out between the neighboring Seneca and Huron tribes, there was an enormous fire in the cornfield.

Lelewala had turned ten that year.

On the evening of the fire, she sat in the longhouse, making cornhusk dolls with her friends, Niabi and Papina. Papina was fourteen, and liked to tell her and Niabi what to do. Lelewala just ignored her, mostly, but when she heard the tribal mother at the door, heard the words '*fire*' and '*lost,*' whispered from the lips of the tribal council elder, naturally, she wanted to hear all of the details, and she told Papina to be quiet. She craned her neck and she brushed her dark hair from her ears, but she still couldn't hear the story. She frowned at Papina, who had grabbed her cornhusk doll, and she snatched it back from her.

"Hey," Papina said.

"My doll's a Jogah." She laughed, and she giggled. "Little Jogah. Jogah. Jogah."

"A *what*?" Papina said.

"A Jogah. The Jogahs are nature spirits. They're small little people that play tricks."

"What kind of tricks?" Niabi wanted to hear more. The girls had forgotten about the messenger at the entrance to the longhouse. The old tribal mother, Gwayeh, was cleaning up around them.

"And this one's a Gagonga. They're stone throwers." She made a growly face, imitated a war with the corn dolls. "They live in rocky riverbanks and caves and they jump out at people and they roll stones down cliffs at them...*Ahhhhhhh!*"

"Lelewala..." Papina rolled her eyes.

"Tribal mother, is that true?" asked Niabi.

The old grandmother, Gwayeh, just looked at Niabi, and she smiled and she shrugged and she continued straightening up around the longhouse. Gwayeh squeezed Lelewala's shoulders and rubbed her back. Then, she brought her some water. Lelewala continued playing with the corn dolls, but she was worried. None of the women had returned yet from the fields, and it was dark now. One by one, the stars were popping. Outside, fires were dying down, rogue fire-flies were winking at her, and faint wisps of smoke like pulled cotton drifted into the longhouses.

"Lelewala, you're always telling stories," said Papina.

Niabi ignored Papina. "Are they always mean—the Jogahs?"

"Not always. Sometimes they sneak around and help people who leave them treats. But they can be invisible."

"Invisible?" Niabi gasped.

"Let's go, Niabi." Papina pulled Niabi away. "These are just silly, made-up stories."

She could tell Niabi wanted to stay and listen as she waved good-bye to her, but she was tired herself.

"Tribal mother, when will my mother be back?" she asked.

"Lelewala, did I tell you the story of the orphan boy whose grand-mother sent him out to hunt?"

Gwayeh hadn't answered her question.

"He was cared for by a woman who had known his parents. When he was old enough, the woman gave him a bow and arrow. Every day, he brought home more and more birds. One day, he knew he could hunt big game and be the greatest hunter in The Land."

Suddenly, she was excited, and she wanted to hear more. The tribal mother was one of the best storytellers in the village. She listened intently.

"One day, he hunted many birds, but as he was going home, he came upon a talking stone. The stone told him that if he gave him half of his birds, he would tell him stories of the world before him. Every day after that, he gave away half his birds and he listened to the stories of the great stone until one day, the others wanted to know why he was not bringing home more birds, for he was the greatest hunter among them."

"I know what happened," she said. "The boy got lazy."

The tribal mother lifted her and carried her to her wooden bed. "*Shhh*...Each day, another boy would go to the stone to listen, and they would pay to hear the stories with a piece of meat or some corn or a squash, until all the boys in The Land were listening, and then you know what?"

"What?" Her eyes were closing now.

"The stone stopped."

Her eyes opened again at once. "That's not fair!"

"The stone was done. He said he was finished and he said that the boys must keep all of the stories as long as the world lasts, and tell all of their children and grandchildren when they visit. From the stone came all of the knowledge we have of the world before us."

She grew drowsy intermittently as she listened, and she whispered, "Storytelling is important, isn't it, tribal mother?

"Yes, little one."

"When I grow up, if I can't hunt, I want to be a storyteller."

"For now, sleep, my dear."

"Tribal mother?"

"Yes, little one?"

"My mother's never coming back, is she?"

In a hushed tone, the tribal mother said, "No, little one."

CHAPTER 3

Many seasons passed, and Lelewala was raised by her father, Chief Honovi, and the tribal elders. She grew to be quite an eloquent young lady, with plenty to say, and she grabbed the attention of many when she spoke. Her brother, however, was not so sure of himself, and though he tried to keep up with the other young men in the tribe, his hunting skills often fell short of his ambitions.

One fall, when the birds were soaring over the rapids of Niagara Falls, and the squirrels were busy squirrelling their loot for the upcoming winter, and the deer were running wild all over Goat Island, the young men set out to hunt. Dyani was sixteen then, but Inola was two years older, and taller than him by nearly a foot. The rapids were fierce where Dyani and Inola marched on, looking for game, singing songs of bravery, until they reached their hunting grounds near Niagara Falls. There, whorls of white capped waves smashed the weathered rocks, rounded all over by the pounding waters, breaking into sea spray and a mist that mixed with the slurry of gravel and sediment that pelted their faces as they stood on the bank.

There they fell silent, stealthily creeping toward the majestic creatures.

"Isn't that the finest buck you've ever seen?" asked Inola.

"Easy for you to say. I haven't even come close." Dyani aimed his bow and he released an arrow, but he missed the buck. The deer ran off. Its hooves crinkled the fallen leaves.

Then, it was silent again.

Inola took skillful aim with his bow and arrow and he split an apple from a tree. Its halves fell toward his pet, a black squirrel named Sallali, who followed him about everywhere. Sallali furrowed her nose and nibbled the apple. Determined to redeem himself, Dyani shot another arrow, this time at a doe. He missed. The arrow ricocheted off an oak, projected into the rapids.

"And now I've lost another arrow," said Dyani. He aimed again, eyeing the buck across the river, leaning too far out over the rapids, but he fell into the water. He grabbed a tree branch, struggling to hold on.

Inola turned around, and at once, he pulled Dyani out of the water with ease, slapping him on the back. Dyani coughed, spit out water, gasping for breath. "Not to worry, Dyani. This island is crawling with deer."

"They practically fall over with their legs in the air for the greatest hunter of the tribe. What will my father say if I come back empty handed again?"

Inola took aim and shot a doe in the rump. "I got her. We'll feast tonight!"

Inola pulled Dyani in a circle, dancing. As he was pulled around, reluctantly, by Inola, Dyani spit out another mouthful of water, and with it a minnow.

"Did you see that, Dyani?"

"Even Heno, the great God of Thunder, saw that one."

No sooner had Dyani said this, when thunder rumbled from above. They looked cautiously to the sky, and to the vortex of mist rising from the falls, where they saw the image of Heno, the God of thunder, appear with wary eyes.

Across the rapids, on the smallest of the three outlying islands, Lelewala walked along with her animal friends—Frekki, a red wolf, Moki, her pet squirrel, and Jaci, a red cardinal who often fluttered about the forest with Lelewala. She had watched as the great hunter, Inola, hunting on Goat Island, hit two bucks and a doe. She stared dreamily now as Frekki, who was dressed in a red coat, boots, and a yellow sash, plunked acorns into the water, splashing Moki. Moki seemed not to notice. He was busy gazing at the black squirrel who was following Inola. Black squirrels were a rare species on the southern bank of the Niagara, and this one was particularly sleek, with a bunchy tail and perky ears that stood at attention.

"Lelewala, if you want that boy to notice you, you've got to do more of this," Frekki said, shaking his rump. "And less of this," he said, folding his hands and bringing them to his reddish-brown cheeks, as he stared off in Inola's direction. He fluffed his tail and strutted before Lelewala. "You need a nice knee-length deer skin skirt and a robe made of turkey feathers. Then you can accessorize with a beaded wampum belt and strut your stuff. That boy will want to marry you in no time."

"Marry me?" Lelewala said, standing on the rocks. "Who said anything about marriage?"

Jaci fluttered up to a tree branch and perched above them. "Lele, you're all dreamy-eyed and, *ahhh!* Like you just saw The Great Spirit himself. I can plan the whole wedding ceremony. Oh, your papa will be thrilled. We'll have squash and beans and corn and—"

"I don't even like corn."

"That's okay," said Jaci, fluffing his feathers. "You can have corn soup." He flew to Lelewala's shoulder and continued where she eyed him, skeptically. "And there'll be dancing. Even Foxy can dance."

"I'm a wolf. A red wolf," said Frekki.

"Sure you are."

Frekki marched around Jaci, He was quite a proud wolf.

"I don't want to marry him. Why does everyone seem to have it all figured out for me? I want to be the greatest storyteller in The Land. Like my mother was." Lelewala dreamed of her mother just then, surrounded by a circle of women from the neutral tribe. Her mother's image appeared before them in the mist above the falls now. She glanced at Inola again and back at her mother's image, smiling, where it dissolved into a prismatic rainbow, and she looked up. "I want to tell tales of hunters and sea monsters and—"

"Of course you do, sweetie," said Jaci.

"I mean it. Tell them, Moki. Have you ever heard of the Onaire monster?"

"The what?" asked Jaci.

"It's a sea monster. It lives in these great lakes and tips over canoes and eats people."

"That's a story all right, girl."

"It's true! And Inola is the most legendary hunter of our time. I bet one day he'll hunt the Onaire, and then I can tell the tale to all The Land."

"And you two would make a great couple," said Jaci.

Then as Jaci hummed *Here Comes the Bride*, Frekki took Moki arm in arm and proceeded to walk, as if they were solemnly walking down the aisle, but Moki scampered ahead a few steps, and he determinedly dug a little hole with his paws. Before he realized it, Frekki, with his nose in the air and his eyes down, fell into the hole.

Lelewala couldn't help but giggle.

"I don't want to marry Inola, Frekki. I just want to tell the whole tribe. No, no—the whole tribal council of all the great Indian nations. Wait—all their children and the spirits of those passed on, too— about the story of the great hunter. I can hear it now." Lelewala stood tall and spread her arms apart in front of her. Then she spun around on the rock and regarded the rapids at her feet. They were so vicious, so unrelenting. Unpredictable. One wrong move too far out into the current, and she'd be swept away. She dipped her toe in the cool water, and she nearly slipped on the covering of moss beneath her feet.

She turned back to face her animal friends. "And I've got more stories to tell. Inola is destined to do great things for the tribe."

Jaci rolled his eyes. "Nah, you don't have the hots for him at all." To Frekki, he said, "Foxy, she's too young."

"That's right. I'm too young to think about things like marriage," said Lelewala.

"No, Lele. You're not getting any younger on that end, girl," said Frekki. He looked at Lelewala, frowning. "You're too young to tell stories. Stories are for old maids."

Frekki covered his paws in dust and he mussed up his red hair, making him look aged and gray. He grabbed a stick and he hobbled along like an old man. "You're a beautiful Indian maiden, Lele. Look at you. And you're the daughter of the tribal chief, just waiting for a man like...like what's his name."

"Inola," said Jaci.

"Inola...to walk into your life and sweep you off your feet and—" started Frekki.

Jaci fluttered excitedly around Lelewala so much that she fell off the rock, into the stream. She splashed them both playfully and she scooped up Moki and she rubbed his head. He purred, stuck out his tongue at Jaci and Frekki.

When she stopped laughing, she said, "I'm an Indian maiden who wants to tell the world great stories, report about my people, and The Land. The Great Spirit."

She tossed Moki into the air.

Moki's eyes bulged, he squealed.

"I still think it's for old maids," said Frekki.

"Storytelling is part of my history." She imagined a picture in the sky, of the amber cornfields and the bountiful harvests of her childhood. Her mother running through the meadows with her.

The great fire.

Her face fell.

"Tell us a story, Lele," said Frekki.

Reluctantly, she agreed. She wanted to show them just how important storytelling was. Not just for her, but for all of her tribe and the Indian nations. She thought for a minute, then she started. "Long ago, the corn sprang up on its own and filled the golden meadows with pearly grain and green husks until Onatah, the Spirit of the Corn, wandered from her fields with her sisters. Before long, Onatah was taken by an evil water monster, and when she was rescued, she no longer had her sisters, the squash and beans, to help her when the fields were dry, or when the meadow was ablaze and needed rain. She had to watch over the fields and never leave them. And once, our village was besieged by a terrible drought. My father's father sent one of his men up the river to find out where all of the water went."

"And then what happened?" said Jaci. He flew higher, around Lelewala, in circles.

Now if you can imagine Moki running up to Lelewala as a television reporter would do, with a little squirrel-sized report, pointing to the rapids, wearing a neatly-pressed jacket and a striped tie, wearing glasses, sitting at a desk with his squirrel fur combed over the side of his head, and a map of New York state posted behind him in the background, this is what the little squirrel appeared to do. He pretended to report the news, with alerts flashing below him, much as they do on television today.

Lelewala simply looked at him, confused.

She continued her story, walking along, describing the water monster in animated detail. "It carried with it the smell of burnt flesh. It glowed radiantly, even as it crept along the floor of the river, burying itself ten feet beneath the surface, and the 226 boils on its back seeped yellow slag that seared the skin of anyone it touched."

Lelewala's animal friends listened attentively and soon, countless creatures had gathered around her from all over the vast forest.

She said, "Once, the Great Creator God Glooskap fought the water monster above the mist."

Frekki grabbed his sword, pretending to fight a monster. With the entire forest crowded beside her to hear her tale, the story had taken on a life of its own.

CHAPTER 4

There was quite a gathering listening eagerly around Lelewala now. Great bears and families of mice, and even the water frogs and nymphs and newts drew close. Soft croaks of warty toads and chirps of cicadas and the buzzing of dragonfly wings could be heard whenever she paused. Her audience was rapt. Across the river bank, the Indian hunters were drawn to the dozens of deer that had crowded around the outlying island.

Inola and Dyani spotted the congregation first.

"What is it, Salli?" asked Inola.

Sallali batted her eyelashes and pointed at once with her paws toward the diverse crowd.

"Dyani, look at this! I've never seen so many bucks in one place before. Why, there are so many, you'd have to try pretty hard to miss one."

Dyani immediately aimed his bow and he took a shot and he missed. He was way off. He blamed Sallali, brushing her off his shoulder. Sallali squeaked a laugh and hid at Inola's feet.

"*Shhhh!* You'll scare them, Salli. Run along girl. Don't start trouble," said Dyani.

Sallali shook her head and her bushy tail and she placed her paw to her forehead.

But Inola was eager. "Come on with me, Salli. I've got to know what all the fuss is about." He and Salli crept closer still, to investigate the commotion going on upstream. They peered through the trees. Salli pointed out the animals and mimicked as though she were storytelling herself, standing on a tiny rock, but Inola was confused.

"You've already got three bucks this morning, Inola. I'm not going back to the village empty handed. This one's got my name on it." Dyani took aim with his bow.

Closer to the gathering now, Inola inched closer.

Sallali tugged on his leg, pulling him back.

A beautiful Indian maiden stood on the rock. Her black hair blew in the wind.

Inola was love struck. He leaned in, lying prone on the grass, peering through the bushes. He watched the beautiful Lelewala—the way her hands gestured when she spoke, her animated expressions, and of course, the enticing words. His eyes widened.

"She's the most beautiful thing I've ever seen," whispered Inola.

Lelewala caught Inola's eye, smiling.

He looked away.

Then, Sallali glanced back in Dyani's direction. Inola moved closer still.

Dyani was taking aim in their direction, but Inola was captivated by Lelewala. Sallali tried to pull him back, but he shook her off, dazzled by the Indian maiden and her following. She was the same girl he'd known since childhood, but somehow, she'd changed. Now she was beautiful and tall and lean and muscular, with limbs that moved with sinewy strength as she perched on the rocks. And her voice was whimsical. "No, Salli. I have to get a better look at her. I want to see her. She's so beautiful...and her story...it's like magic."

"What's all the racket?" Dyani withdrew his bow, distracted by the noises. He grimaced. Lelewala was surrounded by dozens of deer. "Oh, it's my sister."

Lelewala began to tell the story of the stone then, the story that the tribal grandmother had told her about how all of the knowledge of the world had come to be known.

"Lelewala, be quiet. You'll scare all the deer," Dyani called. He had a clear shot now. He aimed at a buck with his bow and arrow through the clearing.

The animals watched Lelewala, unwavering, captivated by her storytelling.

Dyani said to himself, "If I don't hit this one, I'll never shoot another arrow again as long as I live."

He released the arrow and he closed his eyes and then he opened them again. He saw Inola moving closer to the crowd, running. His arrow raced ahead.

It was headed straight for Inola.

"No, Inola," he called.

In a heartbeat, he looked toward the arrow, then at his sister, and finally, at Inola.

"Inola, it's just my sister. "Get out of the way!"

But it was too late. The arrow found Inola's back, piercing through his chest. He fell heavy, saclike, to the ground.

CHAPTER 5

A cross the river, Moki ran to the shore of the island, then quickly back to Lelewala, distressed. He pointed to the fallen hunter with the arrow through his heart. Lelewala saw her brother running toward Inola. The other hunters were close behind him where he knelt down.

"He's...he's dead," said Dyani.

She ran as fast as she could now, out of the clearing and across the foot bridge, and she knelt down beside her brother at Inola's feet, crying. Dyani looked up. His eyes were fierce.

"Lelewala, your storytelling distracted him. I had a clear shot at the buck. Then Inola ran closer and—"

"You don't have to say any more, Dyani. Inola is dead. It's all my fault." She turned her head, shamefully. Then, with Moki at her heels, she turned, and ran off.

"Lele, wait!"

She kept running, as fast as she could, and she hid her face.

Briefly, she looked back. "I will never return to the village after what I've done, brother."

Dyani called after her, "Now, wait, Lele. I didn't mean to be so—"

Sallali pulled him back. Lelewala was already gone. He knelt down again at the fallen hunter's body.

To the little squirrel, he said, "Just like my sister. Why are women so overdramatic?"

To this, Sallali merely gave a *hymph*, turned her head.

"She'll come back." To the mortally wounded Inola, Dyani said, "Oh, Inola. I'm so sorry, dear friend. I can't believe this happened."

He bowed his head and the hunters followed suit, and behind them, the great sun set in red fractals, broken, distorted, over The Land.

CHAPTER 6

Now Lelewala ran toward the river, upstream, where she'd left her canoe. The other animals had gone back to doing what animals do. The beavers went back to building their dams along the streams, the squirrels returned to gathering acorns and chestnuts and twigs—they were expecting a cold winter, and the cardinals and blue jays retired to their nests to feed their young. But Lelewala's closest friends, Jaci, Frekki and Moki, ran swiftly after her, trying their best to keep up with her as she sprinted through the forest.

"Stop. Stop! Lele, will you please stop? My wings are starting to frizz."

"Lele, where are you running off to so fast like the forest is on fire?" said Frekki.

"I can't return to the village, Frekki," she said.

"Now, everybody needs a little time away, but let's be reasonable, girl."

"Right. Right. A little time out might be good for all of us," said Jaci.

"No, Jaci. I mean I can't go back...ever."

It was growing dark now.

The animals cowered together.

The forest at once grew desolate, and night fell, and the ground frosted cold, crunchy. She wanted to be home, too, in the village. She didn't have many friends there her own age—most of the girls thought that she had her head so far up in the clouds that she could talk to the Sky God. And when she rehearsed her stories, they probably figured she was talking to herself, and they looked at her like she was crazy and then they whispered and they laughed and they kept on walking right by her.

But her father was there in the village. Her warm bed was there, and the tribal elders, too, who passed on their knowledge and their stories to her.

She was always ready to hear more stories.

"Lele, that's crazy talk. We'll all—I mean you'll be alone in the forest. That's no place for an Indian princess," Frekki said.

"I've dishonored my brother, Frekki. And the whole tribe. Because of my storytelling, Inola is dead."

Frekki tried to comfort her. "Lele, Dyani loves you. He didn't mean what he said. He just needs time to—"

"No, Frekki. It's more than that. I guess I..."

"What is it, Lele?"

"I did love Inola. I wanted to say it in my own way—in a story, but look what I've done."

"Lele," said Jaci, gently.

Lelewala sat on the ground, crying, with her head to her knees. By now, night had fallen and she made them a fire and the forest came to rest in the way it did when only the sounds of night animals could be heard around them. She could not sleep. After a while, she looked up, solemn, and she reiterated her promise, said, "I can never return."

"But, Lele, we're out here alone in the dark. At least tell us a story," said Frekki. His teeth were chattering. "How about a ghost story?"

"I was thinking more like something with bunnies, butterflies," Jaci said. "It's scary enough out here without adding ghosts into the mix, Foxy."

"The story of Oniate—dry fingers. He's a bogeyman," said Frekki.

Lelewala smiled, and she wiped her eyes. "We could all use a story. Are you sure you want to hear *that* one?"

"Yes," said Frekki.

"No way," said Jaci.

Lelewala drew them in, close to the fire. Their shadows fell on the stone and the trees around them. The glow from the fire warmed the air, their faces. The other animals had long since burrowed to sleep in their dens. The birds roosted in the birch trees, and their soft coos could be heard among them. Then they, too, fell off to sleep, in their nests of maple and elm twigs, and the forest was motionless.

She started. "Dry fingers is the arm of a mummy. It's a spirit that flies around and *punishes* badly behaved people, especially those who speak evil of the dead. It can fly, and any person touched by its withered, dried finger, is struck blind."

Now, in case the little cardinal wasn't frightened enough already, Frekki snuck up behind Jaci, and covered his eyes with his paws.

"*Ahhhh!* My eyes! I can't see! It's got me, Lele!" the little bird wailed.

Lelewala and Jaci erupted into laughter at once.

"Sorry, Jaci. That was mean. I had to get you back for calling me a fox," Frekki said. Jaci turned around and shook his tail feathers in the wolf's nose, until he let out an enormous sneeze. It was so loud that it shook the trees, blowing the embers from the crackling fire all around them.

Then suddenly, it was silent again.

"Great story, Lele, but that's not going to work. I need more of a bedtime story. Unlike Frekki, I'm not afraid to admit that I'm scared out here away from the village, alone, in the middle of nowhere." Jaci's beak chattered.

Lelewala was again sympathetic, and she stroked the little bird's head. "Ok, ok. How about the story of the corn?"

"No more ghost stories," said Jaci.

"He's afraid of the dark," Frekki said.

"Am not." No sooner had Jaci said that when a twig snapped behind him, and he flew off his log and flapped his wings wildly and hid under the canoe. "Maybe a little..."

The fire was dwindling. Moki pointed toward the village, whimpering to Lelewala to return. She started to tell them another story, the story the tribal mother had told her about the history of storytelling, her favorite, although they'd heard it at least a dozen times, and soon, Frekki and Jaci dozed off to sleep.

"Oh, Moki. I can't go back. Not after what I did. I've dishonored my brother, my father, the whole village." She looked around, suddenly aware of the sounds, the cold ground, the pitch dark night. The tiny crystals of ice frosting the grass. Yellow eyes peered out from the trees. She shivered. "I am pretty hungry, though."

A branch snapped behind her.

"Who—who's there?" She looked around, but there was no one.

Then, an owl landed beside her on the log. Moki scurried beneath her feet.

"That'sssss my line," said the owl.

"What do you want?"

"I only wish to help you."

"I'm fine. I don't need any help."

"You *mussst* be famished. Try these." The Owl dropped some shriveled raspberries at Lelewala's feet.

"I don't want any. Go away." Before she could say anything more, Moki scrambled out from beneath her legs, nibbled a berry, and nodded in approval. He held one particularly large raspberry before her, between his paws.

"*Sssssuit* yourself."

"Wait—I'm starving. We've walked all day and night." She nibbled some more berries and she took a sip of water from her canteen and she looked at the owl. "Thank you."

"What's a beautiful Indian maiden doing alone in the forest at night? *Mussst* be a *sssadd ssstory* behind it."

"No one wants to hear my stories. They think stories are for the elders. For the old women of the village. And my stories only cause trouble."

"*Sssounds ssserious*. You need to be the *ssscenter* of your own *ssstory*. Not telling *sssomeone elssse's*, my dear," said the owl. "That's just some wise *advicssse*."

"What do you mean?"

"*Ssstrong* hands and *heartsss* have a life to live, a tale to tell."

You—you sound like someone else. Like a snake, not an owl," she said. Then at once, she wished she hadn't said it, for she knew it was rude. She turned away.

"That'*sss* rude. I'm *jussst* a friend. A wise friend. *Sssomeone* with *experiencssse* in these *mattersss*."

"I don't have a story to tell. I'm not even interesting. I wanted to tell of Inola's great hunting, but now he's dead."

"Everyone has a *ssstory*. Why, do you know how I got my wisdom?"

She was always interested in hearing a new tale. She warmed her hands by the fire and she glanced behind her and she asked timidly, "What—what happened?"

"I grew wise from *experiencssse*, but the *pricssse* was high. The Everything Maker has great powers. He took all of my beautiful features away and banished me from the daytime. I only come out when it'*sss* dark. And I wear a mask, *alwayssss*."

Lelewala swallowed. "That's a great story, Owl. I wish I had something more to say, some lesson to teach. Frekki's right, though. I really should go back and beg for my brother's forgiveness."

"We create our own *hissstory*, my dear. Why, if you went back now, they'd probably expect you to just get married to *sssome sssecond* rate warrior."

The owl hissed, revealing its black tongue, dry and cracked like the veins of broken asphalt. Lelewala drew back. The owl leaned closer.

"Owl, why is your tongue black?"

"*SSSShhhhhh!* That's*sss* a *ssstory* for another time."

"These waters hold a *ssstory* waiting to be told by a beautiful maiden like *yoursssself*. A strong maiden. No men have ever *sssurvived* these mighty rapids and lived to tell about it, though."

Lelewala thought a moment. Then she stood up, and she said, "That's it, owl. I'll ride the rapids. Then they'll have to listen to my tale about how survived the mighty Niagara."

"But what if you never return? These *watersss* are very *ssstrong*."

"No, Owl. I'll do it to bring honor back to my brother, to Inola, and the whole village. Tomorrow morning, I set said in my canoe down the Niagara. This will be my tale."

With this, the owl was pleased, and it told her that it liked her idea very much, and it told her to lie down and to get some rest and to dream of what she was to do in the morning and of nothing else, and it told her that her journey would be a heroic and valorous one that would bring honor to her entire tribe.

And then it flew off, into the night.

CHAPTER 7

That same evening, a full moon illuminated the Onguiaahra village. The air was crisp. The smell of wood smoke filled the air. Outside the longhouses, Dyani paced by the fire, alone. He looked to the sky and he looked out at the distant forest and he looked at the light from the longhouse. Then he walked to the door and he pulled the deer skin tarp back and he sat at the table, where a group of hunters was gathered.

"Dyani, Lelewala has not returned to the village," said the hunter, Kwatoko.

"I shouldn't have been so hard on her," said Dyani. "We have to find her."

"I'll gather a search party right away. We'll search the entire forest."

"Please, don't tell my father. He doesn't need to worry."

The Indian boys looked at Dyani and then at each other and then back at Dyani. They nodded. Then, together, with their weapons in hand, they went out into the night.

CHAPTER 8

Behind Niagara Falls was a vast cave. Not just a small recess of rock inhabited by bats and covered with moss and lichens with a trickling stream of water running through the tortuous cracks in the shale—but a great and massive cave of winds, made of boulders and intricate mazes in the rock and stone rooms hidden by the massive power of the falls. The winds and waters pummeled the rocks and created this ethereal world all its own, apart from the outer gorge.

The cave was home to Heno, God of Thunder, and it was only visible to those whom he wished to see it. On this particular morning, before Lelewala awoke in the forest, Heno had been up since sunrise, wondering what to do about his son, Janok. The boy had no enthusiasm for making thunder, or for much of anything for that matter. His favorite spot was lying on his rock bed, reading a magazine with his feet up, preferably with a snack.

Today, Janok had slept until noon.

Heno entered the boy's bedroom, bare-chested, with his white hair and beard blowing back from the winds that whipped through the caves. He roared loudly at the foot of Janok's bed, and his thunderous voice shook their home. Janok's snoring blew a lock of his dark hair off of his forehead, but the boy otherwise didn't move from his sleep. In fact, he must have been enjoying some sort of dream, because a broad smile spread across his handsome face. Slowly, his eyes opened halfway and he stretched and he rose from the shale slab where he slept. His eyes were still only half open as he meandered down the hall to brush his teeth.

"You don't have to shout, Pops." He yawned, checked his reflection in the mirror.

This displeased his father very much. He was determined for Janok, his only son, to follow in his footsteps, learning to make thunder across The Land. "It's past noon already. You can't sleep the day away."

Janok splashed some water on his face. He walked out into the enormous stone room where all voices echoed, and he grabbed his lacrosse stick. "I wasn't going to sleep *all* day, Pops. I was just thinking I'd go for a swim, play some lacrosse against the rocks..." Janok bounced his lacrosse ball against the cave wall behind the falls, sending a landslide of rocks and debris clambering to the base of the falls.

Heno grabbed the stick. "Will you please stop that? Why don't you take things more, more...seriously?" He roared loudly, and the wind escaping his mouth and blowing in from the falls blew back Janok's hair.

Janok turned his head where his father roared, his jaw dropping. "Pops..."

"How will you ever inherit the throne one day to the God of Thunder? Can you even *make* thunder?"

"Pops, I was about to say…I do take the family thunder business very seriously. It's just I wish I had—"

"What? Is it your voice? Are you ready to practice your booming voice? I know it's been cracking and that's just a part of growing up, son. We can start by working on your muscles to push back the mighty gorge like your old man did." Heno flexed his muscles. He cleared his throat, which shook the Cave of the Winds. "Why, I carved out miles of gorge all the way from Lake Ontario, past the Whirlpool, to this very point, and I did it with one arm. Are you finally ready to learn how to do it, too?"

"Pops, I was actually just hoping for a—friend. Someone my own age."

"You're the son of a God. What use do you have for mortal acquaintances?"

"I can't live forever behind these waters, Pop, without any contact with the outside world."

Heno cleared his throat, and the ground shook, this time more forcefully.

"Of course you can. Before you were born, your mother and I lived here alone for thousands of years." Heno examined the picture on the stone mantle, a classic pose of his late wife. Angelic white hair, wide smile. The photo warmed his expression for a moment. Then his eyes saddened and his brows rose sorrowfully.

Janok looked away.

"Pops, I—"

"If your mother could only see you now." He forced a smile.

"I know exactly what she'd say. She'd say I need to get out of here, explore the world, and take on new adventures beyond this cave of winds full of nothing but hot air. She'd say I need a nice—"

"I won't hear any more!" Heno started toward the door, banging on his chest, but Janok followed.

"A nice girl, Pops."

"That will only distract you from being the greatest maker of thunder in The Land."

Janok sang a song then.

He sang of how, for a long time, he'd been thinking about everything in the world that he wanted to see, and how he wanted to explore the earth beyond the Cave of the Winds, and how he didn't want to do it alone. He tried to explain to his father that he was changing, inside and out, and that he had hopes and desires that he wished he could control, but that he could not. He climbed to the top of the small waterfall hidden in the depths of the cave and he dove into the pool of water beneath it. Sometimes in the winter, it froze, and he sledded down the solid ice with his three sisters. This year, he hadn't been interested. All he could think of was how he wanted to meet someone new, someone his own age.

Finally, Janok's song was done, and Heno spoke. His grumbling rumbled the floor through the sheets of dolomite and limestone and around them through the granitic shelfs. A ray of light broke through the mist, lit up the dark room.

"All right, all right. I see your point. I went through this with your sisters, but I didn't give an inch with them, you know. Let me see who I can pull up in my Rolodex. Here we are...sons and daughters of Gods and Goddesses. What about the Inuit Sky God, Torrigasok's son? You could play lacrosse together."

"A girl, Pops. A girl."

"Oh, right. Right. That boy's got his head in the clouds anyway." Heno laughed. "Get it? Sky God? Head in the clouds. Drum roll!"

Janok was straight faced. "Pops."

"Nothing? Not even a smile?" He thumbed through his contacts. "Tough audience."

"I get it."

"Okay. Okay. Let's see. Who else have I got here?" He looked up. "I've got it! Gagapa, the crow spirit has a daughter. Why, she looks as lovely as her mother."

Heno displayed a picture of the girl. She was lanky, with raven hair that stuck out in all directions, and she had a large wart on the tip of her beak-like nose. Her mother looked even more bird-like, as if she were actually part crow herself.

Now Janok was obviously trying to be nice. He scratched his chin. "Uh...she's friendly, but...I think she's uh...afraid of water. Yeah, that's it. That wouldn't work out so well down here."

"Oh yes, yes, I forgot. I suppose not. Wait. Wait. Hold on a moment." Heno held up a finger, turned away from Janok. Then, a loud thundering distracted him. His voice boomed now. He turned back around. "Janok, I told you to stop throwing that ball against—"

"It's not me, Pops. Look!"

Heno looked, startled. Janok pointed to the mist falling in front of the falls, where the image of an Indian maiden had appeared. She was canoeing down the rapids.

Janok was amazed. "It's—it's a beautiful maiden. And she's telling a story. It sounds so magical."

Heno held up his hand. He began to roar loudly. "Beautiful story! It's a death hymn. That's what it is! No one crosses into my water and lives to tell about it. No one!"

"Pop, wait. Don't!"

"She's almost at the point of no return. I ought to—" Heno roared, causing an earth quaking thunder that rumbled the water.

Black storm clouds gathered outside the caves, simmering a cauldron of electric energy in the sky, and surrounding them, Heno's terrible voice shook The Land.

CHAPTER 9

Just as she had set out to do that morning, Lelewala and Moki had gotten into her canoe and headed down the Niagara. She'd left abruptly before Frekki and Jaci could try to stop her, and she'd paddled around the upper river a while, amongst a cluster of cattails and reeds and sedge grass that grew beside the north end of Grand Island, where birds swooped down in sudden funnels to nest and mate.

Finally, after hours of paddling, she had summoned the courage to brave the rapids.

Once she left, there was no turning back.

As she approached Niagara Falls, storm clouds loomed ominous and thunder rocked the boat from all sides. Around them, lightning electrified the water. The gentle water of the upper Niagara now turned from a crystalline blue and white to a slurry of angry gray.

Lelewala hummed a death hymn to honor Inola, but before long, she started to realize that she was in over her head. The whitecaps on the waves splashed into her tiny canoe, filling the boat with water.

The silvery current nearly capsized it, and she fought against the strength of the waters to keep it on track.

Now, she wanted to turn back.

She felt alone, doomed, and she vigorously tried to paddle to the shore, but each time she came close, she was tossed further into the raging Niagara.

In the sky above the falls, a raven circled, watching Lelewala, as her canoe lurched right and left, adrift in the violent rapids. It followed the river past the falls, past miles of gorge, where the majestic falls had eroded an escarpment of rock cliffs, all the way downstream to the whirlpool where Chumana, the snake maiden, lived. Chumana had once been a quite beautiful maiden, with red lips and long black hair that curled at the tips, just beneath her shoulders. However, for telling stories filled with malice and lies, she'd been cursed, banned from the neutral village. The Great Spirit had transformed her into part snake, so that her locks turned to ferocious snakes when she was angry. He'd given her a horrid looking serpentine lower body which oddly, gave her the strength to swim in the strongest of currents.

As the years passed, she'd learned to control the curse with her black magic, and she could transition between a human and a snake, and many other animal forms. But she'd been cursed with something else, the thing she hated most, the thing she could never hide—a slithery, black tongue. Now it's been said that one has black tongue when talking badly of others, or gossiping, or even bending the truth in a mischievous way, but this was an actual, slimy, black-as-night appendage. It came out of her mouth when she wasn't careful, and sometimes, she had no control over it at all, and it made it impossible for her to hide her true form.

And now, Chumana changed her outward form once more.

She chanted a spell and she threw a fistful of magical dust into her whirlpool and with a loud burst, she transitioned from the owl, who had convinced Lelewala to ride the rapids, into her favorite form, that of an unscrupulous snake woman. She felt most comfortable in her own skin in this way, enjoyed gazing at the boils on her tail and popping them and watching the pus ooze slowly out of the little pustules. She set her snake hair in rollers and she put on her housecoat and her slippers and she put her tail up on her tortoise shell ottoman.

The raven, Kangee, was an evil bird who worked for Chumana. He perched beside her and dropped a magic acorn from his beak into the whirlpool and soon, they both visualized Lelewala in her canoe, careening toward Niagara Falls.

Chumana stroked the raven's head and she kissed it and she asked him to bring her a glass of robin's blood, for she was thirsty after all the talking she'd done with Lelewala. The maiden had taken a lot of convincing, but she'd finally succeeded in her trickery. "Good work, my eyes and ears. Since I was banned from the village, I've had to rely on you to get my information. You never fail me."

"No one wants to hear *sssstories* second hand. It's *heresssay*."

Chumana stirred the whirlpool with her scepter. The image of Lelewala barreling down through the rapids, out of control, appeared in the magical funnel of swirling rapids. Its purple-black water spun faster then. "Look here, Kangee! Honovi's daughter fell right into my trap. He loves her more than his son. She had it all. And the poor girl is throwing it all away."

"*Tsk tsk*. How could she be such a foolish girl?"

"She could've been princess of the village forever, appointing the tribal council, but life is too much for her." Chumana laughed, stirred the whirlpool, and she took a sip of robin's blood from a golden challis. "She'll never survive the rapids."

"*Ssstupid, sssilly, ssselfish* girl."

"Even if she survives the fall, she'll slide right down the rapids and into my—"

"*Ssswimming* pool." Kangee pretended to spin in the vicious current of the whirlpool, until he was soon caught by the force of the spiraling water. He flapped for help, beating his wings as he spun. The water was turbulent, and it pulled into it all sorts of animals and boats and tribesmen that tried to navigate it.

"Kangee! Get out of there!" Chumana held out her staff. The raven grabbed on with his beak, clawing and pulling himself out of the swirling rapids. When he was safely resting on her shoulder, she stroked his head. "Yes, my *ssswimming* pool."

Kangee fluffed his feathers. "She won't swim very well."

"Maybe I should send her canoe this way." Chumana stirred the whirlpool faster, and with her magic, she created a river from it to the top of the falls, one that sucked water inward, to steer Lelewala off her course, and straight to her lair. It was so deep a trench that it could drop the depth of the river by several feet, instantly, harness its energy, its power. "Then I can steal her powers of storytelling that seem to captivate the whole forest."

"Yes."

Chumana stomped her tail. Her snake hair sprung out from the rollers, and her eyes bulged, bloodshot and spidery red. "My stories are just as good. Sure, I might embellish them a little. I might hurt some feelings or bend the truth, but it's all for entertainment! Maybe my tales aren't as virtuous as Eyota's daughter, but I never deserved to be cursed like this—with this black tongue!" Her black snake tongue rolled from her mouth. Her eyes bulged.

Kangee's eyes widened. "*Yesss...sssend* her down a path to our home, and *sssteal* her gift of *ssstorytelling*."

"Yes, I'll steal her gift. And with it, Eyota and Honovi's son, Dyani, will fall in love with me, and with his precious sister, Lelewala, gone, I'll be able to return to The Land, and I will rule every one of the Indian nations."

Lightning flashed mercurial, hitting the water in a jagged bolt.

She stirred her cauldron beside the whirlpool. She tossed a handful of batwings and squirrels' and rabbits' feet and cardinals' feathers into the pot. With a yellow and purple burst of electricity and a flash of fire, she transformed herself into human form. Soon, she appeared out of the water as a beautiful, brunette maiden. Legs sprouted from her lower body, and her massive snake tail receded, but the black tongue remained.

"Be careful. Heno may have even greater powers than you, master."

"Silence!"

She dunked the raven underwater, into the whirlpool, as he clung to a ragged branch of driftwood. Then she pulled him out as he gasped for breath and flapped his wings. The raven squawked, and flew up to its perch. Chumana's staff lit up the water with bolts of lightning zigzagging from its pointed tip.

"Her *friendsss* and family will search for her."

"You're absolutely right. I've got to stop them. Let Dyani and Eyota think she's gone—dead—with no hope of return. Let Dyani live with the guilt of killing both the great hunter and his own sister during the same moon." Her laugh was menacing. "He'll be begging for sympathy and a beautiful maiden to make him feel better."

"Like you." Kangee hissed.

"Now you're just kissing up."

"Be careful."

Chumana extended her snake tongue, coiling it around Kangee, nearly choking him as she laughed at this. He squawked, until finally, she released him. "Not to worry. My magic is strong. And I like this *ssstory* very much."

Chumana swirled the whirlpool faster.

The image of Lelewala faded to that of another—she saw Lelewala's animal friends, Jaci and Frekki, racing to tell the great Chief Honovi, the village, and Dyani, of the maiden's peril.

At once, she realized her plan could be foiled.

"Go! Go now, Kangee! Heno's kingdom of the falls and all The Land must belong to me." Chumana's smile coiled at the ends of her red lips. She licked them with her black tongue. "Take care of her friends, and bring Honovi to me."

CHAPTER 10

Lelewala tried desperately to paddle her canoe against the current, but it pulled her along, closer to the perilous drop only miles ahead of her—Niagara Falls. She was terrified by Heno's angry face in the mist, as they careened down the rapids, now dangerously close to an embankment of rocks. Black storm clouds loomed just above her head, and they poured rain onto her back and into her boat as it smashed against the rocks, jarring her backwards. Thunder cracked all around her, and Moki cowered beside her, popping his head up from time to time to check the course of their fate.

Deer ran from the shore beside the river. Salmon jumped from the white capped rapids, their scales illuminating in the angry sky as the canoe crashed against the stones. Seagulls swooped overhead. Moki's teeth chattered. Lelewala's knuckles grew white as she clutched the paddle.

"Moki, I made a huge mistake. We must go back."

Lelewala frantically paddled her canoe toward the river bank. As she passed the Three Sisters Islands, just beyond where Inola had been shot, she saw a tree just ahead of her. Its spidery branches extended out above the river. It was an old tree—firmly rooted with thick limbs and tortuous trunk roots that knotted and bulged above the ground. As she approached the farthest of the tiny, outlying islands, she twisted her body with all her might and extended her arms above her, grabbing hold of the branch. She clung to it for an instant, but it was wet and slippery, and it snapped loudly, breaking off. She nearly fell out of her canoe as it swept passed the island, her final hope.

Above her, Heno's voice roared. She looked to the sky.

"Why are you in my water, maiden? Are you prepared to meet thy death?"

"Moki, did you hear something?" She looked all around her.

Moki popped his head out of the canoe, pointed toward the falls.

Lelewala tried to paddle backwards, unsuccessfully. She was ready to give up hope, when just as she turned around, Heno's furious face appeared above the mist.

It meant the falls was just ahead.

"Are you prepared to die in my waters, maiden?" boomed Heno's voice, again.

"I'm sorry! The owl—the owl convinced me I needed a story to tell. My own story—one that people would listen to. I made a mistake. It's all my fault. And Inola's death was my fault, too. So I suppose I am prepared."

Moki shook his head, vigorously. He was not prepared. His teeth rattled louder now, over the rushing sound of the water. He stuck his tail out the back end of the canoe, spun it around like a motor, but it was too late. They were too close to the deadly two-hundred foot waterfall.

Lelewala bowed her head, humbly.

Suddenly, Heno was sympathetic. "Owl? What owl?"

"The one with the black tongue," shouted Lelewala. It was difficult to hear over the roar of the water, and over Heno's voice.

Heno roared again, and his anger shook the whole river so that it rose up in waves like the oceans.

"That was no owl, fair princess—that was the snake maiden, Chumana. And her stories are nothing but poison and lies!"

Just then, the boat thumped beneath them, and the muscular tail of a great river monster tossed the boat backwards nearly one hundred yards. Lelewala screamed, and she closed her eyes. When she opened them, Chumana was swimming up beside her boat, laughing. Hot lightning bolts smoldered from her scepter, burning another river off the Niagara, just ahead of the canoe. Chumana knocked at Lelewala's canoe with her snake-like lower body, but Lelewala paddled steadily, staying afloat. Chumana lifted her tail above the water. Then she brought it crashing down, so that it obstructed the river to the falls and soaked Lelewala with an enormous wave.

"Chumana," said Heno, raising a lightning bolt above his head. He threw it at her at once, but she diverted the shock with her electric scepter. Its golden end glowed white hot against the black sky, and it blinded Lelewala's eyes as she tried to steer the canoe away from the snake maiden.

Chumana's tail thumped against the boat.

Lelewala screamed, dropping the paddle.

"That's right, Heno. The fair maiden has a tale, but she won't be alive to tell it. Her story will be mine to tell, and the Indian nations will be mine to rule with my words. They will all listen to me."

"Stop, Chumana. You've gone too far."

Heno roared, and his powers went head to head against Chumana's magic. With his muscled arms, he forced the huge snake out of the way. As their opposing forces of good and evil squared off, Lelewala and Moki were thrown over the falls, disappearing and fading into the mist.

Temporarily defeated, Chumana hissed, began to swim away. She looked back, dodging Heno's lightning bolts, as she slithered back toward the whirlpool.

Heno looked around, woeful, for the maiden in the canoe. "Fair maid of the mist? Oh where has she gone? I'm afraid even the great God of Thunder is too late to save you." Across The Land, his voice boomed, but it was directed at Chumana. "You'll pay for this, snake maiden. Stay out of my waters. Let everyone who hears my voice beware. Stay out of my waters!"

Thunder split the air in a deafening crack. Yellow lightning crackled against the purple-black sky, and as the sun set, Heno faded from the mist, returned to the Cave of the Winds.

CHAPTER 11

Deep in the forest, now miles from the Niagara, Jaci and Frekki frantically ran for help, back toward the Indian village, searching for Chief Honovi. Kangee flew ahead, and with a mischievous smile across his beak, the raven clotheslined Jaci with a branch, knocking him flat onto Frekki. It was quite an abrupt fall—stars circled above both of their heads.

"Have you *lossst* your way?" Kangee asked.

"What? Where am I? Where am I going?" Jaci fluttered around, still confused.

A large lump formed on Frekki's crown. He rubbed it. "Wait! I know you. You work for the snake maiden."

"I'm only a *messsenger*." With his beak, Kangee offered a satchel of raspberries to Jaci.

Jaci snatched them up. They'd been travelling for two days now with little food.

Frekki slobbered as he spoke, grabbed the satchel of cheesecloth containing the berries. "Don't touch those! They might be poison, like Chumana's words. Her stories are full of lies and gossip and, and..."

"The snake maiden may have valuable information on the Indian princess, Lelewala."

Frekki grabbed Kangee by the neck, still slobbering as he spoke, but the raven turned his beak away. "Are you telling me you know where Lelewala is? Is she safe?"

"Chumana is the only one who knows the *ssstory* of your friend. It'*sss* a good *ssstory*."

Frekki released the raven from his chokehold. "She's got black tongue! You can't believe a word that witch, that...that snake creature says. And if she's done anything to hurt Lelewala I'll..."

Jaci nipped at Kangee's tail feathers now, but the raven flattened him with his wing. The cardinal struggled to get loose, and finally he flew free and he settled on a branch overhead. Frekki drew his sword, which weighed nearly twice as much as the little wolf. He swung it wildly at Kangee, back and forth, almost severing his head, but the raven dodged it. The dense sword seemed to have a mind of its own in Frekki's paws, and after he had exhausted all his effort, he took one final swing at Kangee, missed him altogether, and lodged the weapon in the trunk of an oak tree.

"Calm yourself, *Foxxxy*," said Kangee.

"I'm not a fox. I'm a wolf!" With this most insulting comment, Frekki flashed his sharp teeth and swallowed Kangee whole, but the raven pushed the wolf's jaws open with his broad wings, standing inside his now wide open mouth. Kangee tried to speak, protesting.

"Let me out, fox. Wolf. Whatever you are. Or you'll never find your friend," shouted Kangee.

Frekki spit out the raven, burped up several of his scraggly feathers. "Is Lele alive? You better start talking, you old bag of feathers."

"Come *sssee* for *yourssself*. The whirlpool holds great truth for those who look into it directly." Kangee sprinkled a golden dust over an apple, transforming it into a crystal ball. It grew to the size of a pumpkin, and clearer than a harvest moon. It displayed an image of Chumana's whirlpool, swirling tirelessly. Then it flashed white, then golden, and it showed Lelewala barreling down the rapids, but Kangee quickly covered the hologram with his wing. It quickly disappeared and turned back into an apple, now rotten, which fell to the ground at Frekki's feet. He examined it, glaring into in from every angle and trying to make the vision reappear. It remained a soured, rotted fruit.

He tossed it back to Kangee.

Then Frekki chased Kangee around the oak.

"Truce! Truce!" Kangee squawked, came to a halt. "That'*sss* all I can show you...*Jussst* a *tassste*." Kangee bit the apple. "But the snake maiden has magical *powersss*. She can show you much more in the whirlpool. You *mussst* gaze into it."

"I'm not going near the whirlpool. There's imps and devils and spirits in it. It'll suck me in." Jaci pranced around, looking like a devil, making pointed horns with his paws.

Frekki said, "I'll go."

Jaci shook his head.

"We have to see," said Frekki.

"You can't. She'll drown you in it. People never return from the whirlpool. It's a trick."

"We have to see where Lele is," Frekki insisted. He shook Jaci, slobbering again. "I'm a wolf. I can swim. I can fight. I'll just take a peek."

"*Yesss, jussst* a peek." Kangee hissed, turned to leave. He settled on a branch and he tossed some dust at Frekki, who started to follow him, Frekki's eyes now enchanted by the raven.

"I don't know Foxy," said Jaci. He pleaded, "Snap out of it." He shook his tail feathers at Frekki's eyes, hovering around him in the air.

Frekki came out of the trance.

Kangee scowled at the little cardinal, blew more of the golden dust from under his wing, into Frekki's face. It moved through his body, like some invisible force, its energy and radiance penetrating right through him.

"You know what I'm gonna do?" said Jaci. "I'm gonna get the Chief." With that, Jaci started whistling, and he took off toward the Indian village.

Frekki followed Kangee, once again entranced by the raven. Under the bird's spell, he proceeded straight ahead, with his eyes wide open, but his gaze miles beyond him in some parallel world that did not exist except for in this daydream created by the raven, from which there was no awakening.

As he flew away, Jaci called back, "Be careful, Foxy! Don't get too close to the whirlpool, and don't eat any fruit—not one blackberry!"

A moon cratered ivory rested close to the horizon as night fell on the Indian village. Chief Honovi had gathered the tribal council inside the longhouse. Beside him were his closest advisors: Nihol, Kwatoko, and Kohana. They were all skilled hunters, and they had witnessed Inola's demise. Dream catchers of twigs and blue and red wisps of feathers of long ago dead birds hung from the ceiling, and the smell of wood smoke and the frost of autumn leaves filled the air.

The council took their seats at the table.

Honovi was covered in deerskin and wearing a traditional head-dress. His nose and chin were strong in profile upon his face. He stood with his arms crossed, his fortitude apparent. Tonight, he addressed the council with remorse.

"Members of the council. It is with sorrow that we have lost the great hunter, Inola," said Honovi. "More worrisome, we are expecting a terrible and ferocious winter. How is our food supply?"

The council bowed their heads.

Kohana spoke. "We have only the deer that the great one killed before his death. Our food supply is sparse, Chief Honovi."

Honovi rose to his feet. "No one person shall starve. If we starve, we starve together."

Kwatoko had another concern. "The Iroquois and Huron tribes remain at war. We need reserves if we are forced into war."

Then Kohana asked Honovi what he thought of their war, and he asked him why these men fought now, when previously, things had been static like the river and the sky, and Honovi told him that he could not be the judge of the Iroquois or the Huron or even the white man, and he said that he thought of their battles much like he thought of Niagara Falls. Honovi said that he cared not for their motivations but only for their position on the landscape relative to theirs. He reminded Kwatoko that the falls pushed back a little each year, carving the mammoth gorge, ripping stone from stone and defining the path of the river over time, and that it only appeared to be static, because its course was predictable, and nothing could be done to change it now or ever.

Honovi reminded them, "We are a neutral tribe. The Onguiaahra must preserve our namesake, the neutral ones, as long as we can. Kwatoko, are we even prepared for war?"

"I fear the worst. We are not," said Kwatoko. "The drought of summer has left the land barely arable. There is little corn. Even less beans and squash. And we have only today's kills for meat. I fear a long, frigid winter is due, and even the animals we hunt are famished and gaunt. Without another great hunter among us like Inola, surely we'll never survive the months ahead."

Kohana asked, "What about the white man? Inola's strength and stealth protected us from his assault. Twice I've seen explorers looking for the mighty Niagara Falls. Once they know of its power, the word will spread among them, and we'll be vulnerable to attack."

Nihol, who had been patiently listening until now, said quietly, "I too, fear the worst, Chief Honovi. And where is your son, Dyani? His name means deer, but he hasn't been able to shoot one in months."

Voices grumbled in agreement.

Honovi placed his arms overhead, urging the council to settle down. Calmly, he said, "It will be difficult, but we will remain strong.

The Onguiaahra tribe is resilient, and steadfast, like The Land itself. You're correct about my son, Dyani. He is not as skilled as Inola was. But he is brave of heart, and he perseveres. He will come through. The tribe will survive."

Nihol started, "But chief—"

"That's enough," said Honovi. "Remember, the soul would have no rainbow if the eye had no tears."

The tribe nodded solemnly.

At that time, Jaci came flying through the deerskin tarp covering the door of the longhouse, never slowing, until the little bird flew smack into the back wall of the longhouse, and then fell to the ground. Chief Honovi looked to the council, and he shrugged. Then he bent down and scooped up the small cardinal, skeptically. The bird's red feathers molted from his rear, and he perched, quivering, on Honovi's finger.

"Well, well. Every bird loves to hear himself sing. What have we here?"

Jaci shook out his tail feathers. "Chief, Chief—you must come now. Lelewala's run off, and the snake maiden's got her! She's gonna drown her in the whirlpool and—"

"Snake maiden? Chumana's been banned from the village," said Honovi.

The bird was frantic. "Lele ran off, and the snake maiden tried to trick her. Chumana transformed herself into an owl because Lele wanted to tell great stories, and Chumana convinced her that sailing down the river and over the falls was a good idea. Chief, you gotta come now and—"

Jaci was hyperventilating, puffing up his wings and feathers so much that he couldn't get any more words out. Honovi pinched his beak shut, but he continued to squawk, expanding like a stressed puffer fish. Finally, the chief let go.

The cardinal continued. "She's got Lelewala and she's going to drown her in the whirlpool!" he finally announced. He fluttered around Honovi, panting for breath.

Honovi looked concerned, but calmly, he said, "Slow down, little red bird. Why in the world would Lelewala run off?"

"Lelewala was telling her stories when Inola was shot. I told her storytelling was for old maids and Dyani scolded her and she was crying and—"

Honovi pinched Jaci's beak again, and once again, his body ballooned. Another handful of red feathers molted to the ground. To the council, Honovi said, "Then Dyani knows she's run off. That's where he's been. He's been keeping this from me, and that angers me very much."

Honovi placed his bow and arrow on his back. The council rose from the wooden benches.

"Where are you going, Chief Honovi?" asked Kwatoko.

"I must find my children, and feed my people. Talking accomplishes little. We must act. If Dyani cannot hunt, I will for us myself." His voice had something like wrath in it now. "And let Chumana know this: If both of my children are not found safely, I'll skin her alive, and I'll choke her with her own black tongue."

"We'll come with you, Chief," said Nihol.

Kohana said, "We will not waste time."

To Jaci, Chief Honovi leaned in close, and he said, "My daughter's storytelling is virtuous and diverse and powerful. Although Lelewala is young, her knowledge provides a foundation and understanding in our culture." Then he addressed the council with his arms outstretched. "It is part of our history in which both children and elders take great pride. Storytelling writes our past, while it lives the present, and preserves our future. Let no man, woman or animal shame another for telling the stories that are the heart of our Indian nations."

Jaci quivered before the chief. "Y-y-y-yes, your Chiefliness."

"We must find them. And see that the black tongued snake maiden's malicious lies never poison this village again."

Upon hearing these words, the council yelped, and they shouted their war cries where they set out. They cheered so loudly that all of the men and women of the neutral village came running out of their longhouses, into the dark of night, to see why there was so much commotion.

CHAPTER 12

D yani led a team of hunters that same night in search of Lelewala. His men combed the fall foliage, and they searched beside the river, and in caves, and through the forest, all along the rocks of the lower Gorge. It had been a steep climb down, and one of the men had almost slid to his death into the whirlpool, otherwise known today as The Devil's Hole, where rapids crash below two hundred foot cliffs. When Dyani had safely reached the bottom, Sallali poked her head out of his arrow pack, which he carried strapped to his back.

"Lelewala! Lelewala!" Dyani called.

"Dyani, we've searched day and night. It's no use. She's gone."

Dyani kept looking. "Lelewala, it's Dyani. I didn't mean to scare you off. Please come home to the village."

"Dyani..."

Dyani advanced on the rocks, toward the rapids. Then he turned back suddenly. "Wait—I hear something."

Sallali covered her ears, shaking her head. The raging water drowned out all but the loudest sounds.

"You hear what you wish to hear, but it is not as it is," said the hunter, looking down.

Dyani, too, bowed his head.

It seemed hopeless that they would find Lelewala now. She had never been out on her own in the forest. She did not know how to hunt or fish. Food was scarce, and the woods went on for miles. He looked at the gooseberry bushes beside the river, shriveled and picked over by rabbits and deer. Even the fish seemed to hide in the water's reflection, safe from capture. Chestnuts, which normally fell amongst the pinecones and leaves, were sparse there. Still, he couldn't give up hope. He had to keep searching.

"She's here. I know it. I can feel it," said Dyani.

"Your father will be worried about you, too, when he realizes you're both gone. We must return to the village. It's night, late." The hunter placed his hand on Dyani's shoulder.

"You go back. I'm not returning until I find my sister."

Dyani wept. The hunters looked at each other, and then back at Dyani. They nodded. Dyani walked further along the river, alone, over slippery leaves of elm and maple and the browned nettles of coniferous spruce, over slabs of shale, and when he looked back, the hunters had already started the climb back up the treacherous Niagara Gorge.

Sallali peered out of the arrow pack. The little squirrel was quivering.

"Go ahead girl. I wouldn't blame you if you ran off on me, too," he said.

Sallali purred in frustration, and she hopped out of the pack and onto Dyani's shoulder and she snuggled against his chin. He smiled, rubbed her head.

"I have to keep looking." He parted tree branches from his way, and he tore the limbs of thorny brush plants away to forge a path. "Lelewala! Lelewala!"

His voice echoed, but there was no reply.

CHAPTER 13

Heno and Janok paced the lower river in the mist, near the roaring falls, overturning rocks and digging through the rubble at the base of the Horseshoe Falls. With his neck inclined toward their top, nearly 200 feet above him, their superior rim of grey blended to an aquamarine, and then to its infinite veil of white power which crashed down upon them, unrelenting. And there Heno stood in the mist, surrounded on three sides in this colossal equine footprint of a horseshoe belonging to the Clydesdales of giants. Behind him, the mass of Niagara Falls' gallant rapids carried swiftly away the fallen waters. He raised his hands to the sky, pious himself to those Gods above even him, and he thundered, as his face was pelted with mist so thick that he could not see the great Falls themselves before him, nor their tops aloft, his kingdom, his world entire. Only a white blur of their gale beat down upon his face, and he passed through their curtain of white froth, disappearing behind them into his cave, concealed once again in their aqueous fray.

Janok was pacing there. "Where did she go, father? The maiden—the maid of the mist."

Heno placed his hand on Janok's shoulder. "I'm afraid we're too late, son."

"No, I have to search for her." Janok started toward the entrance of the caves.

"You mustn't leave, son. Our home is behind this falls. Our job is to make thunder. Lightning. To guard the falls. Not to chase after foolish maidens."

Now, Heno may have been angry at himself, but he acted in frustration. The great God of Thunder began throwing up lightning bolts and dragging clouds into the sky like it was a touch screen. Retreating to his lair, he pinched and zoomed away the fluffy cumulus clouds on his sky palette, replaced them with gloomy gray wisps of stratus.

"You could've saved her," said Janok.

"She sealed her own fate by listening to the snake maiden. And now her tale is told."

"No, I don't believe that. She could still be out there." Janok grabbed his knapsack and parted the waters, left the entrance to the cave.

Heno followed, protesting. "Just where are you going?"

Janok turned. "I have to look for her, Pops."

"There's no way she could've survived going over these falls. These rapids are deadly. I see to it myself," Heno shouted.

"Then it is your fault. I'm going to find her. She looked lost—like she was running away from something."

"I can assure you, son, she is dead!"

"You don't know that! I'm going."

Heno roared loudly. The clouds assembled in a spinning swirl, and even the fish cowered in the water beneath the overhang of shale slabs cut meniscal in their profile as if sickled out by the hand of death. The billows of green foliage growing out of the rock now overturned their leaves, whipping them upward with the drafts of an incoming storm. Heno shook his finger. "Janok if you leave here. I'll...I'll..."

"You'll what? Not let me back in the Cave of the Winds? Pop, I'm almost an adult. I want to go. It's time I did. And if it means I won't be a thunder God one day like you, then so be it."

Heno slumped down on a bed of limestone, looking defeated. He expelled a heavy sigh. "Oh, I'll...I'll be here when you get back. But be careful."

He parted the clouds, and the leaves rustled, and he revealed the sun so that Janok could see clearly, so that if there was any chance at all of finding the maid of the mist, even a small chance, he might do it.

CHAPTER 14

Janok spent that night in the forest, his first night ever away from the cave of the winds. His legs pained him, and his father had told him that it was due to the pain of growing, for he had grown nearly a whole foot in just a year. Sleeping on rocks and sticks worsened the pain in his bones, and he had no notion of how to build a bed or prepare a meal. At home, his three sisters had done most of the housework. His shirt had perspired with sweat throughout the night as he slept. This was an entirely new sensation for his body. And his voice still cracked high, in wide, embarrassing notes, each time he spoke aloud. Everything in his life seemed out of his control at that time—all the more reason he had needed to get out of there, even if he never found the beautiful maid of the mist.

Despite his need for freedom, he was starting to think that his father was probably right about there being no possible way the girl could've sustained a fall over Niagara Falls, when right at that moment, he spotted her. She was lying face down on the riverbank. A bunchy-tailed squirrel lay on its back, across the maiden's torso. A carpet of seafoam the color of birch beer swirled about the river, like effervescent whorls of cream soda shaken, spilled, washing inward toward the river bank.

When Janok first caught sight of the maiden, he wept, for he was certain that she was dead, and he thought it all his father's fault, but then slowly, she started to stir. Her chest was rising and falling, not just with the undulating water, which gently washed the algae away from her prone form, but with a rhythmic, regular rise and fall—she was breathing. Upon seeing her move, even the slightest bit, Janok came running along the rocks toward the bottom of the gorge. He slid and he fell awkwardly along the gravel, twisting his awkward limbs, but he rose swiftly and he continued running, as the princess straightened her legs and rose to her feet.

The other thing about his body that he couldn't control well during those years were his feet. Not only had his voice started to break and crack at the most inopportune times, but he presently felt too tall for his trunk, tripped often over his lanky legs.

"Fair maiden. You're alive. I've found you." Janok's voice rose several notches now as he spoke. He covered his mouth, embarrassed.

"Who are you? Who am I? What happened?" The maid of the mist looked around as she stood, looking entirely confused. As she tried to walk, she stumbled and fell.

The squirrel beside her whimpered, spitting out a mouthful of water.

"It's okay—don't get up. You're too weak. You took a long fall."

"Fall?"

"What's your name, fair maid of the mist?" Janok asked.

"I—I don't remember. How did I end up here?"

Moki was always rather timid around strangers, and he squeaked into Janok's ear. Twice Janok had to ask him to repeat himself, for his own hearing had been damaged by all the booming and thundering that was the nature of his father's work. The deafening rumbles had left him with a constant ringing in his ears.

"Lelewala? That's your name? That's a beautiful name. And your friend—his name is…"

Moki whispered to Janok. Then he ran behind a rock and he peered out fearfully.

"It's okay, little guy. No need to be shy. My voice is squeaky, too."

Janok's voice hit another high note and Lelewala smiled and Janok blushed.

"What happened Moki?"

While Moki rarely spoke, he was quite the actor. He donned a pair of aviator goggles, and quite similar to the Red Baron flying a plane, he buzzed around Janok and carried on as though he were once again braving the rapids, not mentioning of course, that he had been cowered in the hull of the canoe for the great majority of the ride over the falls. Then he feigned falling, hitting his head, and lying there all bandaged up in bed with a Red Cross symbol pasted across the gauze bandage and a thermometer in his mouth, with one eye black.

Janok was amused. "Moki, that's quite a detailed story. I see your memory hasn't been affected, little fellow, though I'm not sure I follow."

Moki held up a little trophy now, and he took a bow and he gloated a little, for it was his moment, one could say. The rapids roared with applause. Flower petals fell at his feet.

Janok explained to Lelewala, "It happened like this. First my father saw you in your canoe, and then the snake maiden, she came and tried to steer you down the river into her deadly whirlpool."

But Lelewala shook her head blankly.

"Nothing? You don't remember any of it?" Janok scratched his chin where the slightest touch of facial hair was beginning to grow.

"I don't remember." Lelewala said. She stumbled along the rocks.

Now Lelewala couldn't really be sad at this point, because she had no memory of who she was or what she was missing. The one thing that remained of her past, in her mind, was that she had a natural predilection for telling stories. As hard as Chumana had tired, she had not been successful in ripping away Lelewala's gift for storytelling when she had fallen from Niagara Falls. It seemed Chumana had succeeded in stealing away part of Lelewala's memory, but the natural urge to communicate through words was apparently an innate part of her nature that could not be taken by the snake maiden. An intrinsic property as elemental to her matter as the radioactivity of polonium and radium and uranium, bursting forth alpha and beta and gamma rays from atoms hidden in fractals of pixelated matrix, deep within both the tiniest of graveled pebbles and the most immense of the gorge rocks.

And Lelewala's enthusiasm was bursting.

Now, more than ever, she wanted to share her stories. This urge was thriving so much within her that she had to let it out somehow, and so she started to sing, first about the beauty in the forest, and then about the elements of life—earth, wind, water and fire.

She sang of many stories, and Janok asked her if she still remembered how to gather food, and if she knew how to make a fire, and she told him that she did. They sat on the rocks a long time until her mouth was dry from telling stories, and she took a sip of water with her hands cupped from the river, and she told some more. Janok said that his favorite story was the one of how the chipmunk got its stripes by a monstrous bear with claws sharp enough to carve stone, holding it down by its tail as it tried to scamper away. Moki cowered as Lelewala spoke, but she cuddled him close and she told the squirrel that she would protect him from all of the ferocious animals of the forest. Then she sat a moment on the rocks and a little red bird perched beside her and she told Janok that she wanted to tell him a story about the rocks and about the bird's red breast and he said that he'd like that.

"Once, a great warrior, Kluskap, realized how much wisdom an old maid, Nukumi had. He wanted to learn all that he could from her. She said she'd be happy to be his grandmother and to share her wisdom with him, but she told him she was an old woman and she needed to eat."

"Did Kluskap bring her some plants and berries?"

"No," said Lelewala. "She said she needed meat, and could not live on only plants and berries."

"Well wasn't she picky," said Janok, listening intently.

"Kluskap asked Robin to fly to the place where lightning strikes, and to bring the sparks that were there to her. Robin flew to the place, but he had to use two dry sticks to carry the sparks because they were so hot. As he flew, the wind caused the sticks to burn, and his breast turned red. Still, the little bird brought the sparks so that they burned, created fire." Lelewala batted her eyelashes. "This is why all robins have red breasts, and when sticks are rubbed together, they make fire."

"Was the grandmother happy?" asked Janok.

"Yes, because the first meat was cooked over fire, and Kluskap and his grandmother started their time together during which she passed on much knowledge to him."

Across the river, the French explorer, Etienne Brulee, and a dozen white men peered through the brush. The shale tilted earthward in polygonal shapes at the sharpest of pitch where they navigated the terrain, through dogwood and maple trees and sumac branches that concealed their red sashes, and their white cotton shirts and their black leather boots where they crouched. Whimsical notes of Lelewala's sweet voice carried across the north facing cuesta, where the rock bed had not eroded evenly. The men watched, captivated, with their mouths sunken, as Janok lifted Lelewala and carried her off upstream, splashing through the water and the lower rock, where harder layers of shale and dolostone were laid down in a prehistoric sea.

In the lands where the explorers were from, many tales had been told of Niagara Falls, but no man had discovered it and returned safely to tell of its magnificence. Brulee's men drew closer, for they were desperate to find the great falls, and they had travelled for months. Now, a chunk of caprock plummeted toward the rapids where they came to a narrowing, creating dangerous eddy currents and undertows, and where the uneven middle and lower Silurian soft layers of shale eroded in uneven beds and contained within them the ancient fossils of creatures preserved and millions of years dead. As the rock made a loud splash, Brulee stepped back behind a large poplar tree, a mature hardwood with tumorous growths abounding from its trunk. There, he hid from the Indian girl and boy.

Brulee whispered. "Did you hear that, men? It was the best tale I've heard yet! Write it down. We'll share these stories of the creation of all things when we return home."

Brulee's assistant followed him, scribbling notes on paper. "Yes, sir. Wait until the king hears of our tales on the Niagara."

"Of a maiden fallen from a mighty waterfall. The adventure! The danger!"

Another Frenchman shook the water from his boots, spoke. "But sir, we've yet to find the mighty Niagara Falls. We've been traveling for two months. Perhaps it's only legend, as her stories are."

The Frenchman standing behind Brulee had a rifle strapped to his chest. He scowled and he spat and he counted golden coins that clanked and reflected in the sunlight back to his eyes, and he squinted. "We're broke. And there's no civilization here to speak of. Our men are starving. We've risked our lives and our fortunes and we've found nothing."

Brulee was enamored with Lelewala, as many men and women were. "Nonsense, we're close! I can feel it. And that maiden—she's sure to lead us to it. I've never met a woman with such a zest for life—for storytelling."

"Sir, you haven't met her. You heard the boy talking to her—she doesn't even know who she is, sir. How will she tell us of the Native tribes or of the legendary Falls of Niagara?"

"Nonsense! Follow that maiden. There's a magic in her words—in her story! Stay close on her trail. She's sure to lead us to Niagara Falls!"

"Yes, sir," said the Brulee's men, reluctantly.

Brulee slapped his young assistant on the back. "Isn't this exciting, chap? We're writing history as we speak. There are stories to be told. Onward!"

Although Lelewala, Janok and Moki, weren't aware of their presence, the white men followed closely behind them, all the way to the falls. Lelewala sang weakly, though, as they grew closer, until her words trailed off into a whisper, and then they stopped altogether. The waterfall did not stimulate her memory as Janok had hoped, and finally, he set her down. At the end of their journey, she could not stand, but rather, she fell down in exhaustion beside the thundering waters, and she lay at Janok's feet.

"Lelewala!" Janok fell to his knees at once, beside the girl.

"I feel so weak. Too weak to walk, even. I must rest. Please, just go away. Leave me alone."

"No, you'll die here. I must take you home. My father can help."

"Your father?" she asked.

"Heno, the God of Thunder is my—" Janok's voice cracked, and he turned away and he blushed. Then he cleared his throat and faced Lelewala. "Heno is my father. Hard to believe, I know. I've got big shoes to fill. That's part of the reason I left home."

"Left where?"

"We live behind the falls. Here, in the Cave of the Winds."

"But I can't walk. I'll—"

"You don't have to. Don't get up. I'll help you. I promise I'll help you." Janok picked her up and carried her off again with the little squirrel trailing just behind them, but she was so defeated by her near brush with death that she fell asleep in his arms. He parted the horse-shoe waters of the falls where they encircled the two of them, moving them aside as if they were a curtain hanging loose in the breeze. With Lelewala hung over his right shoulder, he walked beneath the falls, revealing the intricate hidden home in the cave of the winds.

Heno sat waiting with his arms crossed.

CHAPTER 15

F rekki followed Kangee through the forest, crossed a clearing
near the whirlpool, and stood on a red pedestal of rock. Birds
that devoured only the corpses of the dead circled above the treacherous waters, but Frekki's gaze was transfixed on the raven. From
there, he looked on at the whirlpool below, gulped, and then the
trance was at last broken, and he remembered why he had come.
Birch and hemlock and knotty pine trees waved them through the
windy narrowing, between the carved layers of compressed rock,
some looking as old as the earth itself. Chumana appeared out of
the whirlpool.

Frekki drew his sword.

Chumana's reptilian tail bulged, sprouting boils filled with a vis-
cous gel that seeped yellow into the surrounding water. Then the appendage receded, and the elegant human legs budded in its place.
There was a smell of rotted flesh and moldy leaves and decaying wet
wood, submerged and washed up on the shore many times again.

"I tell you to bring back the chief and a hunter, and you return
with a meadow fox?" said Chumana.

Frekki growled, baring his teeth. "What have you done with Princess Lelewala?"

"This young wolf was very *concsssserned*, my lady." The raven rested on his perch, a dead tree of rotted wood and wiry branches.

"Thank you," Frekki said.

"*Concsssserned*, I see. Well I don't want to be impolite. Come closer. I *sssupose* you'll never believe anything I say unless you have a look for *yoursssself.*" Chumana approached the whirlpool. She swirled her staph about the frothy sea foam atop the swirling blue green waters, creating an image of Lelewala lying on the riverbank.

"You evil witch! Is-is she dead?" Frekki's voice trembled. From his throat, a knot rose and fell.

Chumana laughed. "You didn't really think she'd survive a tumble over the mighty Niagara Falls, did you?"

Chumana hissed, and she morphed her lower body back into snake form. Snakes sprung from her skull. She coiled her tail around Frekki and she knocked him into the whirlpool and she submerged him. After some time, she pulled him up for air.

"Help! Help! What do you want from me?" the wolf cried.

"You're of no use to me fox, wolf, whatever you are. Bring me Chief Honovi or his son, and I'll help you find your precious princess."

Dyani had been waiting, there, beside the whirlpool, hidden in the sumac, for the right moment to attack, and he now aimed his bow, poised to shoot Chumana. "Stop, snake maiden. You don't have to look any further to find me. I came looking for you."

"Dyani, help!" called Frekki.

"Frekki?" Dyani dropped his bow now and he dove into the water and he swam toward a weathered branch overhanging the riverbank and he broke it off and he offered it to Frekki. "Grab on, quickly."

"Oh, look. It's the not so mighty hunter, Dyani. Looking for your beloved sister?"

"What have you done with her?" To Frekki, Dyani said, "Grab it! Hurry."

Chumana batted at them with her tail, missed. She stirred the whirlpool with her staff, which was now glowing a hot purple-white color. Its tip sizzled as it pierced the water. The whirlpool spun faster. Evil fishes and sea creatures horned and sharp-toothed and charred long ago by fires of hell rose from the sea foam, little holograms swarming the air. They bit at Dyani's ears and nose and dug their knife-like fingernails into his skin. When Dyani swatted at them, they faded to blackness, as if they'd been imagined figments of his mind. He scratched at his skin where it felt like they were still crawling on it.

Chumana hoisted them out onto the river bank, onto the sheets of rock at the bottom of the Niagara Gorge, nearly drowned, and dripping wet. "Where's Lelewala?" she scoffed. "Are you having survivor's guilt?"

Dyani stood and he raced for his bow and arrow, and he picked them up out of the sediment on the shore and he aimed and he shot Chumana in the tail, but she only hissed. Kangee and Chumana's pair of evil raccoons pried it loose at once.

"I—I hit something! I hit her!"

Chumana's laughter rippled the water in large undulations. "Your pathetic wild shots have nothing on me!"

"Did you see that, Frekki? I actually hit something! I knew I could hunt."

Frekki whispered to Dyani, "That's swell, boss, but she's still alive."

"You're making me angry, and anger makes me more powerful." Chumana's tail swelled where the arrow had pierced her thick skin, and she grew larger, meaner, and uglier. Wild tufts of gray hair grew from her ears. She bent the arrow around Dyani's neck and she pulled him closer to her with it. She stirred the whirlpool, faster, and Lelewala's image materialized above it in a glowing white sphere, resembling a crystal ball. "Now look into my whirlpool, very closely."

"No! Lelewala can't be dead! I refuse to believe it." Dyani stared at the hologram. "There—see! She breathes. There's hope."

"It's not looking good for your sister."

"Take me instead, snake maiden. Please save my sister."

Chumana knocked Dyani and Frekki back into the whirlpool with a thump of her tail. After they gasped in the spinning funnel of water, Chumana smiled, and a burst of light shot from her scepter, macabre firework imbued with evil alight. Instantly, the hologram turned to blackness, and the swirling whirlpool turned to a gentle froth of seafoam. Dyani and Frekki floated on their backs and they spat and they coughed and they swam, flailing, to the shore. Chumana's raccoons, her supplicants cloaked in black masks of damp fur, raced toward Dyani and Frekki. The raccoons bound their wrists and dragged them atop a large bed of stone.

"Maybe we can make a deal," said the snake maiden.

"Anything. Just tell me where my sister is. I'm not going back to the village without her."

"Oh all right. For a price, I can tell you where she is, but it will be no good to you." She examined her green fingernails that curved into C-shaped daggers. "The little drama queen has angered Heno, God of Thunder, and she'll never tell another story again."

"There might be something I can do. Tell me, please."

Frekki could hold it in no more, and he struggled with his wrists bound behind him, and he screamed, "You're a selfish old witch. And that's why you were banned from the village. You're telling more lies."

Dyani clasped his bound hands over Frekki's mouth, shaking his head. Chumana's eyes widened and bulged with anger, and she grew larger. She picked them up with her snake tail, held them over the whirlpool.

"My dear creature. Everyone deserves a second chance." Chumana dropped them abruptly onto the shore, and a landslide of rocks and pebbles tumbled down onto Frekki's head from the gorge above. She hissed at Dyani, and her menacing yellow eyes bore into his. "If I tell you where to find your sister, I want to return to the village without this, this, black tongue. One hundred percent human. No tail. No tongue. Just a beautiful, buxom brunette..." Now she smiled and she licked her lips and she pulled Dyani close to her face and flatly, she said, "bride."

Dyani and Frekki cringed, looking away.

"My father will never allow it Chumana. No one wants you there. You know that as well as I do."

"My schmoopie pie, you're hurting my feelings, and being very rude." Chumana swatted them into the whirlpool again.

"Get us out of here. We'll drown. We'll—"

"You're right, Dyani. We'll need to convince the great Chief Honovi that I can be *trusssted* again."

"We?"

"It will be tough. I'll admit. But if you and I were married, he'd have to forgive and forget, wouldn't he?"

"I'd never marry you, Chumana. You're a snake. A—a monster! You're disgusting!"

Chumana submerged him with her slimy tongue. Dyani struggled beneath the surface of the water. His cheeks blew up as he held his breath, and he dug his nails into her snake tongue, kicking and struggling.

Frekki bit Chumana with his sharp teeth, and she screamed. "*Arghh!*"

Chumana released her grip. Dyani and Frekki swam violently to the bank, treading water with their wrists bound.

"You ought to bite your own tongue, snake maiden," said Frekki.

"Why do you want to return to the Indian village so badly anyway?" Dyani asked.

Chumana licked her lips end to end, where they curled. Matter-of-factly, she said, "Whoever tells the stories, influences the world. Don't you see? I can rewrite history as far back as creation, any way I want to remember it. Don't think for a minute that the present can't influence the past. I assure you, it can."

And with that, Chumana wrapped them with her snake-like lower half, and she placed them in a canoe. Her evil raccoons began filling the boat with rocks, one by one.

To Kangee, she whispered, "Once I'm in the village I'll get rid of Dyani, and then his father. A freak drowning accident on a canoe trip—an aquatic escape to the bottom of the lake! No one will suspect a thing, my pet."

Kangee smiled, plunked more rocks into the boat with his beak. The canoe began to sink.

"Not a thing..." the bird said.

By this time, Dyani and Frekki were terrified, and felt that not only was there no way to save Lelewala, but that they, too, would soon perish at the hands of the snake maiden. Chumana mocked them, and she sang a frightening song about how history is told. She said history is remembered by the ones who tell the story of it, and that everyone else's version of what really happened is soon forgotten. Then she hissed and she licked her lips and she told Dyani that perhaps they could make a deal.

"No one would believe I'd marry a snake like you. You're literally...a snake!"

Smaller snakes bulged from Chumana's skull, and she spat poison from her tongue that dissolved the ancient limestone at her feet, sizzling into porous depressions. "There's always the other option, but you won't hunt many deer at the bottom of the whirlpool."

"Be reasonable," Dyani said. "Your stories won't influence anyone if they're all lies."

"I disagree. How about a scenic cruise on a shale raft?"

"Fine, Chumana. You win. I'll marry you. You can return to the village. I'll inform my father of it. But I must find my sister first."

"I don't *trussst* you. I want the marriage license signed in your own blood."

Dyani swallowed, and he looked at Frekki and he looked at the scroll that Chumana had carved into a great oak with the mucronate scepter. It blazed her name into the tree. Scorched chunks of crackled bark flew around them.

Frekki tried to stop Dyani. "Don't do it. She tricked Lelewala. She'll trick you, too."

Dyani looked away and then he looked back and then he pricked his finger on Chumana's staff and he set his thumbprint by his signature on the oak. The blood red leaves of the majestic oak crinkled, fell to the ground, and it withered and it shrunk by a whole foot. She peeled and zapped off the scroll with her staff, transforming it into golden paper. Then she rolled the scroll and she hugged it close to her breast.

Dyani said regretfully, "It's done. Now where's Lelewala? And don't tell me any of your malicious lies. Your gossip. Tell me the truth."

Chumana laughed something intense, loud, enjoying her guffaw from the pit of her stomach. "I'm terribly hurt, lover boy. Give me a kiss." She licked her lips and she stuck out her tongue.

Dyani turned his head, disgusted. "Don't come near me."

She spun around, slightest by the insult. Her eyes glowed yellow. "Heno, The Thunder God, has taken Lelewala behind Niagara Falls. Even if you find her, he'll never let her return to the village. And I'll be the one telling the stories to the children. Stories that will keep them up at night!"

"Chief Honovi will never allow it," said Frekki. "You just keep talking."

"My sweet little fox, he'll have no choice, because I'll get rid of him, too. Without his daughter, I'll be the Indian princess, married to his only son. I'll rewrite the history of the elders, the whole Indian nation, and of all those who explore The Land. She who writes history, controls it!" She waved her staff, bringing up demons and devils from the whirlpool that began to dance around her cauldron.

Frekki cowered.

Enraged, Chumana continued, laughing.

"I'll color the news of The Land any which way I want. Soon, The Great Spirit himself will listen to me!"

CHAPTER 16

Janok carried Lelewala right through the mighty Niagara Falls as if its tumbling fury was an illusion concocted by Heno himself. He parted the waters as they pounded the rocks beneath them, proceeded through a labyrinth of stone caves and pathways to his home behind the falling water. At this point, Lelewala was still unconscious. She breathed heavily on Janok's chest as he set her on the dolomite, weathered smooth by erosion millions of years before. There, she slept beside one of the beautiful water falls within the hidden caves, its mist glistening down upon her skin. The wind howled viciously at the entrance of the falls, a noise which was sure to scare off any man or creature who might otherwise think to explore the void behind them, but the noise turned to a spritely tinkling, and then faded to a quiet whistle, as they approached the center of the palace, where the sun broke through from above.

"Father," called Janok.

"What in the name of The Great Spirit?" Heno dropped his cappuccino, his favorite beverage, which he claimed gave his voice rumbling power.

"Father, I found her—the maid of the mist."

"I see that. She sure ain't the maid of Pskov Rimsky-Korsakov." Heno began to sing an opera. "That's my favorite o-per-a!"

Janok was not impressed. "You really need to get out more, Pops."

"Yes, well." Heno cleared his throat. "Just what do you intend to do with her?"

"She needs help. She's very weak. She can barely stand." Janok brushed Lelewala's dark hair from her eyes. She looked helpless, like a child.

"Well she can't stay here. She's a mortal. We are Gods!" Heno roared.

"Because of you, she nearly died!"

"She got in her canoe by her own free will." Heno turned away.

"The snake maiden tricked her. And you're both so stubborn."

"What's done is done!"

"You have to do something, father. Help her. Let her stay with us. It's lonely here. I've no one to talk to, to trade stories with about our history. No one knows what we do here. And she's such a wonderful storyteller. I feel like we could talk for hours, like I can tell her anything." Janok looked at the sleeping Lelewala, and he sighed and he brushed another lock of her brown hair off her face, but she did not awaken.

Heno grumbled. "Oh all right. I can make her a potion that will restore her strength, but it will only last as long as she remains with you here near the falls. If she goes off again foolishly, before long, she will weaken...and die."

"Really, Pops? You can do that?" Janok was suddenly hopeful. His eyes brightened and he thought for a moment that he might kiss the beautiful Lelewala, but he decided against it just then. Instead, he grasped his immense father with all his boyish strength, hugging him and spinning him around.

"After all, what's my name?" Heno winked and he examined his fingernails. "I am a God, you know. I know we live under a raging water fall, but did you really think your old man was all washed up?"

The little squirrel, Moki, who had quite a sense of humor, made a drum roll sound. Heno looked for laughter or applause or a smile from Janok, but Janok was serious and straight faced, shook his head.

"Come on, Nothing?" Heno asked, hanging his head in disappointment.

"Oh, there's one other thing, Pops."

Heno raised one of his white eyebrows hopefully. He seemed to be starting to like the idea of the maid of the mist coming to live with them. "You forgot to tell me about her widowed mother? An older sister perhaps? I get lonely, too, you know."

Janok grimaced. "No, Pops. That's just weird. It's that she— doesn't remember a thing before the fall."

"Oh?"

"Nothing. Not where she came from. Where she was going, or how she got there—nada."

"Maybe that's for the best, son. My powers can only do so much. Let's see what I can do..." Heno began to mold a waterspout from the fallen water. It turned into a gargantuan ball of spinning water in an instant. Then it burst into what looked like crystals of sunshine, into a fine mist that sprinkled down onto Lelewala.

Heno himself seemed quite surprised at his own power, and he and Janok regarded each other as if to ask what had just happened. They both shrugged. Then Heno continued, and he raised up the water into a funnel that veered right and left around the caves, sucking the river dry in parts. When he was done, the sun came out, and a radiant glow, saturated with colors, appeared to rain down from all of the water falls surrounding them. The behemoth Horseshoe Falls turned to a brilliant red that blended into yellows and greens as it crossed over to today's American Falls. Even the tiny Bridal Veil Falls was a lovely blend of blue and indigo. The colors bent and twisted until a huge rainbow stretched out across the entire sky, covering the region from end to end.

Heno said, "Behold. The rainbow is a sign from Him who is all Things."

"You mean you didn't do that last part, Pops?"

Heno shook his head.

"The Everything Maker, The Great Spirit," said Janok. "But is she?"

Moki ran over and tickled the skin just beneath Lelewala's chin with a tiny buttercup. At first, she didn't stir. But then, as the little squirrel continued, she could no longer hold back, and she burst out laughing and her eyes opened and she sat straight up on the rock.

Heno breathed a heavy sigh. "The fair maid of the mist lives! Welcome, fair maiden. Welcome."

"Lelewala, you're alive! And you're strong," said Janok. "Can you walk?"

Lelewala regarded him very strangely now. "Why wouldn't I be able to walk?"

"Your memory—do you know where you are?" asked Janok.

Lelewala appeared to be thinking for a moment, and while it was a miracle that the girl was even alive, it seemed even more remarkable that her memory might have returned. After a while though, she said, "Not a clue. But this place is amazing! It's like we're behind Niagara Falls."

Janok and Heno glanced at each other, evidently deciding on who would be the one to let her in on the little secret behind their magical location.

"We are," Janok said. "Lelewala, this is my father, Heno."

Lelewala coughed and she smoothed her deerskin dress and she fidgeted with the red feather in her hair. She started to braid and twist it, looking around nervously as Moki snuggled at her heels.

She laughed. "I don't think I heard you correctly, Janok, because for a minute there I thought you said your father is the God of Thunder."

"It's okay. Don't be scared. He rescued you after you fell from the falls," Janok said.

Janok looked at his father for guidance. Moki imitated paddling and falling.

She scoffed at this suggestion. "That's ridiculous. There's no *way* I could survive a fall over Niagara Falls. Why, it's almost 200 feet high!"

Janok felt it best not to press the young girl. "Maybe your memory will come back to you. In the meantime, you can rest here. Regain your strength."

"I'm plenty strong." Lelewala chuckled and she hopped onto a wooden swing beside one of the tiny falls, and she started to play. Then she jumped off and she ran and she spun around under an even smaller waterfall. "It's beautiful here, Janok. I'd love to stay, but I have to get...home."

No sooner had she spoken the word home when she stopped, quietly. She turned and she faced Janok and Heno and she asked, "Janok, where's my home?"

Heno reminded him, "She can't go. She'll only keep her strength while she lives in the mist."

"Pops?" Janok asked.

Heno explained, "I'm a God, I'm not a sorcerer. I did the best I could."

Janok looked at Lelewala and he shrugged sheepishly as he knew he was hiding this one little thing from her now, and he was a remarkably terrible liar, which spoke well of his character. His voice cracked as he spoke. "While you try..." He cleared his throat from its high note and he continued. "While you try to remember, we'll take care of you. My sisters love to cook, and they'll fix your hair, your clothes, your room—whatever you need. Your wish is our command." Humbly now, he knelt down, and he said, "I think you'll like it here. Please stay."

Janok led Lelewala into the caves with his arm in hers and she looked rather unsure, but she followed, for the unfortunate girl had no other option. Heno's daughters, three of them, came out of their elaborate rooms now and they sang a song of welcoming. They'd been spying from their doors in excitement, and now they couldn't contain themselves a moment longer. The three daughters were all fair, with different hair colors that hung below their elegant shoulders. They ushered Lelewala past Heno's golden throne, to an elaborately decorated bedroom that sparkled and gleamed where the sunshine peeked through the enormous ceiling. Stalactites pointed their giant spears of limestone downward above her, and a private waterfall glistened in the center of the room, and a stream followed its course out of the caves and toward the falls.

Ava, the youngest of Janok's sisters, a fiery red head, led Lelewala up a curving staircase embedded with stunning pieces of blue-green sea glass, to the top of Niagara Falls, where she pointed to the breathtaking view from their patio. Lelewala had never been so close to the falls.

She stepped back, grabbed her chest.

Tons of water plummeted earthward every second, and it filled her with a certain anxiety, but she could not say why, and yet no memory came to her of her fall.

Ava plucked wisps of mist from the falls as they rose like translucent cotton, up toward the heavens. She shaped them into clouds as one would shape a ball of dough, and she blew them, with a kiss, back into the sky, and she told Lelewala that she would have endless fun helping her make clouds, and she told her that sometimes, she shaped them like animals and other shapes just for fun, but that she couldn't do it all of the time because she was afraid that their home would be found if she did it too often. Lelewala was about to try her hand at cloud making when Ada took her hand and pulled her away.

They slid down the banister and Ada pulled her into the kitchen. It was filled with all of the foods she suspected a god might need for nourishment, including nectar and honeysuckle and fruits and vegetables she had never heard of, but ones she had imagined in her dreams like watermelon and cantaloupe, and there were more strawberries and blueberry bushes than she could count. Her mouth watered. She was famished and she wanted to try all of the delicious fruits and shove them in her mouth all at once. She had only popped one raspberry into her mouth—although it was a delicious raspberry and just ripe, when Agatha now insisted she see her wardrobe.

Agatha, well, she tried to dress everyone in the highest fashion, but her efforts fell short of her ambitions at times. She tossed garments out of her armoire, a supreme feature of the establishment, thirty feet high with spirals and shelves carved of granite by Heno himself as a present to his daughter. Ada and Ava grimaced as Agatha pulled a purple cloak of velvet around both of them and spun them around. Then she forced her own large feet into a pair of green slippers, singing off key about her love of dressmaking, as she wound her blond hair into a knotted chignon. Lelewala, wanting to be a polite guest, simply smiled, though she was fortunate when Janok finally appeared at Agatha's door.

Lelewala stood speechless. She wanted to join in their song, thank them for their hospitality, for she would otherwise be homeless and alone in the forest with Moki, and while he was a charming and loyal companion and always by her side, she couldn't expect a little squirrel to hunt, or to protect her from the elements, or from the grizzlies and coyotes and wolves and other wild beasts of the forest.

Lelewala hopped on the swing beside her bedroom falls and she swung back and forth and then she jumped off and Janok caught her and his voice cracked when he said, "Welcome."

She sang that she wasn't sure where her home was, and she sang to the sisters, thanking them for their kindness, and then she sang, "I'm going to like it here."

Somewhere inside her, though, something was missing.

CHAPTER 17

Near the whirlpool not far from Lelewala, Chief Honovi and the members of the tribal council searched desperately for the lost maiden. They cut back grasses that grew up past their knees and they forged a trail through an area that grew barren as they advanced, as if there had once been a scorching fire there. As they approached the whirlpool, the vegetation that was green and vibrant and fruitful dropped off to a pathway of charred and carbonaceous branches, trampled and half broken and seared to ash and gnarled with webs of driftwood and washed up sea moss where few plants now grew.

There was a gnashing of teeth from animals never before seen by man.

As they approached the whirlpool, these animals with teeth like knives and cataract eyes jaundiced and coursed tortuously with spidery red vessels peered out at them. A twig snapped, and the men turned.

It was only Jaci.

The little cardinal flew ahead, located Dyani and Frekki. Then he whistled and tweeted as he hurried back to the chief.

"*Shhh!* Red bird, silence. I hear someone."

"Maybe it's the white man," said Kwatoko.

"Why must you always be so negative?" asked Nihol, shaking his head. "Maybe it's Lelewala." He called out, "Fair maiden! Are you there?"

Honovi placed his hand on Nihol's shoulder. "Nihol, *shhh*. You are a strong warrior. Brave. Resourceful. But it is better to have less thunder in the mouth and more lightning in the hand."

The warriors nodded in agreement and proceeded with caution, cracking the lifeless branches and leaves as dead and dried of life as the fossils of the millions of prehistoric arthropods compressed in the massive rock corridor surrounding them.

Out of nowhere, Chumana poked her head through the water of the rapids. The warriors jumped back. A cloud of blue smoke clouded the air as she rose up from the seafoam on a floating throne of iron.

"Less thunder in the mouth. Funny, I was just saying the same thing to Heno," she stared at Honovi and laughed. "Right before I sent Lelewala over the falls."

He regarded her with smoldering eyes, drew his bow. "Chumana."

"Don't you mean daughter in law? Your son and I just had ourselves an old fashioned wedding. I'll be returning to the village as Dyani's bride. That means you can return me to my true form...one hundred percent human." She puckered her lips and outstretched her human arms, expecting a hug.

They coughed as the smoke cleared to a misty haze, and Dyani and Frekki became visible beside the water, where Chumana had imprisoned them.

Honovi withdrew his aim. "The way of the trouble maker is thorny, snake maiden. I returned you to your true form years ago. Instead of speaking, why don't you listen or your black tongue, or it will make you deaf, too."

Chumana glared at her reflection in the water, the snake like lower body, and her black tongue. She pressed her hands to her cheeks. "No, it can't be."

"It's true. The reflection you see is who you are. Your true self. The spell upon you has been undone for years." To Dyani, Honovi called, "Tell me she lies, son. Her words cannot be true."

Dyani tried to explain, but the chief wasn't known for his patience. "I'm afraid it's true, Father. Chumana wishes to return to the village as my wife. And I only wish to find Lelewala. I made a pact with her, so she would reveal Lelewala's location."

Perhaps Chief Honovi wasn't thinking straight on that autumn day, because he erupted into a fit of rage as soon as Dyani had gotten his words out.

"Lies! More lies. If it's true, then both my children are dead to me. If I banish you, too, from the neutral Indian village, then neither of you will return. You have dishonored me by abandoning your sister. And now she is gone forever."

"Father, we can find Lelewala."

"Now you dishonor me by conspiring with this monster. I banish both of you from the Indian nation!"

"No, father. I did it to find Lelewala. She's still alive. I know she is. She went over the falls not far from here."

"Silence! If she's fallen from the mighty Niagara Falls, it is impossible. My daughter is dead."

Chumana smiled, and she looked sideways at Dyani, licked her lips. Her black tongue snapped back, recoiling into her mouth. "I tried to tell him."

"Father, this can be undone. I promise you."

Chumana hissed. "Read the marriage license for yourself, Chief. It's written in your son's own blood." She held the scroll, signed in Dyani's blood, for Heno to see.

Honovi turned away at once. Then he sat on a rock and he put his head in his hands and the warriors watched him silently, and when he stood up and faced Dyani, he said, "I am a fair chief. And to you, Dyani, a patient father. You have contributed little to the tribe, but your intentions were always sincere, until now. Smart frogs to not drink up the pond in which they live. Now, you wish to poison and destroy things with your lies, like Chumana, so you, too, must suffer the consequences."

Honovi sat on a great slab of limestone and he crossed his legs and he held his arms to the sky and he began to chant to The Great Spirit, calling upon the little demons that Dyani knew of only in his imagination, through Lelewala's childhood tales. She had spoken of the malicious gnomes and dwarves as if they were frighteningly real, and perhaps he had chosen not to believe in them, despite their place in Indian legend. Now his father was summoning the mystical creatures as his accomplices. The earth started to shake, and the Jogahs and Gagongas appeared from the dark shadows of Chumana's lifeless lair.

Dyani looked all around him at the miniature cliff dwellers. They stared down upon him, a menacing brood. Despite their diminutive stature, their eyes glowed with the orange and yellow pulsation of slowly kindling firewood. They were covered in a thick mange of gray fur, save for their leader, who was hairless from top to tail, and their foreheads were broad and horned.

"Father! What's happening?" Dyani called.

"Oh, Great Spirit. Let everyone in The Land know of this woman's destruction. She's taken both my children from the village. If it is your will, see to it that she do no more harm."

The pygmoid Gagongas now tumbled rocks down onto Chumana. Her agile body dodged their insults at first, laughing. Then the earth quaked, stronger, and the walls of the Niagara Gorge grew higher, encroaching on the evil snake maiden. The stone throwers made huge splashes, and they hurled larger boulders now that created rippling tides as they splashed into the river below.

"Dyani, what are those creatures?" Frekki asked.

Dyani struggled to loosen his wrists where Chumana's raccoons had bound them. "Jogahs. Gagongas. Lelewala used to tell stories of them when we were kids. I didn't think they were real."

"You think you can destroy me with elves, Honovi?" She looked to the sky, and she laughed. "I've got an army of my own!"

Chumana's leathery tail swelled, and she swatted away the Jogahs from the rocks as they climbed down further into the gorge, pelting her with shale. They ascended the rocks as quickly as they fell, and they merely snickered, continued their assault.

Chumana was infuriated now. She smashed her tail down upon The Land, causing a powerful tremor so large that it knocked the Indians to the ground, and tilted the escarpment rock laterally even steeper than one million years of evolution had done thus far.

"The stories told by Lelewala and the legends of our people will live on. Even if my daughter is gone!" Honovi turned and bowed his head, looking defeated in spite of his anger.

Chumana rose higher out of the water on her floating throne. Her obese tail and pannus cut an ominous shadow on the shale walls surrounding them, and she summoned her demons now, whose spears in their trajectory upward toward the stone throwers narrowly missed Dyani's heart more than once. A massive boulder careened from the Gorge above him. The Jogahs were throwing balls of fire now, which sizzled and hissed as they grazed the dewed ferns and plunked, hell bound, into the water.

Dyani covered his head and dodged the debris and the blazing rubble sliding down the rock wall. When he had loosened the restraints and freed himself, he grabbed Frekki, and he ran for his life.

"Father, please stop this," he shouted.

But Honovi bowed his head, and continued chanting.

CHAPTER 18

I n the Cave of the Winds behind Niagara Falls, Janok and his three
sisters sang and danced and feasted with Lelewala. Agatha had
dressed Lelewala in a rather ostentatious red and yellow dress of col-
ored deer skin, a buttery suede adorned with beads and feathers and
horn buttons. Lelewala much preferred her simpler attire, but she
was a good sport and she thanked Agatha graciously for her hospitality. Ava's cooking was suffused with aromas of divine fruits. There
was moose and deer meat cooked to perfection that was smoked
and fell from its bones in her mouth. She ate and danced with the
troglodytes in this terrestrial cave until somehow, she felt at home,
like she'd been a cave dweller herself, lived there for one-hundred
years.

Lelewala naturally told stories, and the sisters traded tales of
their youth, and this banter continued all evening, until the five of
them were drunken with delight, and a sudden rattling interrupted
them.

It was Heno's phone to the Everything Maker. Heno picked it up,
stepped away from the feast.

Lelewala was quite comfortable and a bit giddy now when she said, "Oh, Janok. If I never remember where I'm from or where I'm going, I hope I—"

"I hope you always remember me." Janok finished her sentence.

They were about to share a romantic kiss, despite Janok's sisters leaning in dreamy-eyed, doting, watching, but Heno interrupted, stepped back into the room.

"Hold on, son. I'm getting a call from upstairs. Chumana's causing more problems in the Gorge. Gotta go to work." Heno hadn't noticed his son's display of affection, or maybe he had ignored it. He pulled Janok aside, away from Lelewala, urgently. "Let me show you how this is done. I've got orders for a terrible storm. First, I throw up some ominous black clouds."

Lelewala watched intently, as Heno moved the clouds about, as though the sky in its panorama was his movie projector, and he, the director. "Can you do that all by yourself?"

Heno raised a white eyebrow. "What's my name?"

"But isn't it dangerous?"

"Sweetheart. I'm a thunder God. It's what I do. I go big and they go home. Now watch."

Heno then dragged lightning bolts, and a white-purple glow lit the cave.

"Yeah, Pops. Isn't it danger—" Janok's voice hit a high note. He repeated, "Dangerous?"

"Son, when are you going to step up? If you're going to be a thunder God, you've got to learn from your old man."

Janok stepped up to Heno's cauldron. Heno pulled lightning and storm clouds out of the iron pot, but Janok looked quite hesitant and unsure of his abilities. An electric yellow serum crackled, boiled over the cauldron, dripping storm scum and sizzling onto the serrations of rock in their hidden vault. The limestone dissolved where the acid seeped around their feet, and Heno sang a song of thunder and lightning.

Around them, the sky turned pitch black.

CHAPTER 19

The lightning that Heno threw down upon the river crashed into the water of the gorge, illuminating the waters. Honovi and his warriors fought back Chumana there. Vultures circled above, and screeched in shrieking sporadic calls for flesh rotted and dead. The wisps of marshmallow cirrus turned at once to anvils of cumulonimbus with long flanking lines, leading towering storm clouds.

"Father, what's happening?" called Dyani.

"Kangee, get away from there!"

Heno's lightning splintered an oak where Kangee sat, perched and preening his ragged feathers. The raven alighted against the purple sky where an electric spectacle of his plumage fell in all directions. He squawked and fell to the ground.

Chumana looked to the sky, dodging falling rocks.

"Oh, Great Spirit," Honovi chanted.

Chumana retreated, swimming away to the lake.

"This is Heno's doing!" She swam further from the storm, calling to her pet, "Kangee, get up! Let's get out of here—quickly!"

"Be gone, snake maiden! Swim out into the lake with the other river monsters, or I'll finish you off once and for all," Honovi called.

Dyani held Frekki under his arm and dashed away, narrowly missing an enormous falling boulder. When he was safe in the distance, he looked back at his father, who had bowed his head in sorrow.

CHAPTER 20

Four seasons changed along the Niagara River. And after that, Lelewala circled the sun three more times. It was spring time then, and Lelewala and Janok were out one morning near Goat Island, exploring the Three Sisters Islands, which where a gift of bountiful thanks from The Everything Maker to Heno for dutifully protecting The Land near Niagara Falls. Lelewala steered their canoe through the waters between the islands, coursing carefree through the twists and turns of the stream. She barreled down a dip in the river and she came around some large burgundy-colored rocks, laughing as the fresh water splashed at their faces. She was quite confident in her canoe these days. Moki rode on her shoulders, frightful, as the little squirrel always was.

"Easy, Lelewala! We don't want to get you too close to the falls. Remember what happened last time," said Janok.

Lelewala looked away, and she slowed the canoe and she brought her paddle down into the water to steady their course.

"I'm sorry. I forgot," said Janok. He brushed a wisp of Lelewala's hair from her eyes. "You don't remember."

"It's been four years."

Janok pulled the canoe off to the side of the river bank and he took Lelewala's hand and he helped her step out of the canoe. "My father doesn't like me showing off. Let's take a walk over here."

"You say I fell over the falls, but I still don't remember."

"I shouldn't have reminded you. You had almost forgotten."

"No, Janok. I never forget that I've forgotten. I think about it every day. I wish I knew where I came from—who I am."

"Let's walk around these islands. It's said one can hear the voices of spirits past here. Maybe it will refresh your memory."

A whimsical gust of air tinkled, blew through the trees, and their hair stood on end and made their hearts beat faster.

"But it's been so long. You don't really believe that, do—"

Before Lelewala could protest too much, she saw something— an image. It flashed before her eyes in an instant, in succinct but clear pictures, of an Indian warrior, his bow drawn, and its arrow released, racing towards a definitive endpoint.

It faded just as quickly.

Then, another flash.

She saw the arrow, its accidental target—a warrior taken to the earth, fallen with a leaden thud by the mortal wound of the arrow.

Janok touched her arm. "Lelewala, you look like you've seen a ghost. Are you okay?"

"Yes, I'm fine. I think."

Janok skipped a stone, and in Lelewala's mind, its bouncing trilogy of ripples on the glass stream flashed red-orange images of Dyani, the deer, Inola. A trout leapt parabolic and splashed in the aftermath of the stone's throw, and the water muddied and it cleared and so did Lelewala's vision.

"When I was little, I used to come here and play. My three sister's and I had contests who could throw the farthest. I always won, of course." Janok smiled proudly. "Sometimes I'd hunt deer, but only when no one else was around to see. It was pretty lonely, and these islands are crawling with deer."

"Hunting…" repeated Lelewala.

"Lele, what is it?"

"I just thought I saw something. A deer. A hunter, maybe."

"I knew it! Your memory. It's coming back."

"No, no. It was nothing." Lelewala turned from the sun where it radiated brightly through the leaves, its corona breaking through in patches of white. "I—I want to go."

"But you saw it yourself. You're starting to put together the past. I knew these islands held a magical power."

"Maybe I—I don't want to remember anymore. This is my home now. I'm happy here. It might be too painful to leave—to return to another time and place. Maybe I wasn't even happy there. Maybe that's why I left."

"You don't have to leave, Lelewala, I love you." Janok looked around. Then, happily, he roared, making thunder.

Lelewala looked at him. He was no longer gangly and awkward, but had grown into a handsome young man who had come of age. His back was muscled and his jawline chiseled. His form now had the strength of a leonine beast painted on an ancient cave wall, and it was difficult for Lelewala to remember the awkward boy that he once was. He looked around at the birds who were tweeting to him and looking on. He had, in fact, surprised himself with his call.

"Did you hear that? My voice—it didn't even crack."

Lelewala smiled. "We're not kids anymore, Janok. I love you, too."

Janok got down on one knee, and he looked up, and he took Lelewala's hand. "Will you stay here with me always? Will you be my bride, Lelewala?"

Lelewala glowed, said, "Yes, Yes, Janok."

Janok stood and he leaned in to kiss Lelewala. She closed her eyes. Just before their lips met, Lelewala saw another image that this time, her mind couldn't shake.

She pictured an owl with a tortuous, elongated, black tongue. She pulled away from Janok's embrace.

"What is it?"

"Let's go back to the Cave of the Winds," said Lelewala.

"Then I'll tell my father of our intention to be married."

"Yes, let's hurry, Janok."

Janok took her hand, splashed through muddy waters filled with salmon and scaled trout. They ran down the spiral of rock stairs over petrified loess, away from the canoe, all the way to the base of the falls. Morning glories bloomed before their eyes, and the sun beamed on them as they ran. Lelewala glanced over her shoulder, still enchanted and shaken and consumed by the visions.

Across the river at what is today Canada, the raven, Kangee, spied from the highest branch of a knotty maple tree, tapping the delicious syrup from beneath the bark with his beak, and licking the liquid and crystalline clumps from his claws. He called out as he now flew off in the direction of Chumana's lair, as the sun set blood red in the west, on the falling water.

CHAPTER 21

Later that evening, the Tribal Council: Honovi, Nihol, Kohana, and Kwatoko, convened around a small fire in their longhouse. Rings of wood smoke rose through the hole in the ceiling, and particulate wisps of ash blew about in the air and fell to the ground. Jaci sat on Honovi's shoulder. The proud bird wore a tiny headdress of his own now.

"Members of the tribal council. It has been three years since my daughter's disappearance. It is with great sorrow that I say we must resign our search," said Honovi.

The council members were solemn.

Nihol said, "There's always hope."

"That is true. But we must address the concerns of our neighboring tribes," said Kohana.

Kwatoko looked toward the chief. "Lelewala may still be alive. And Dyani—"

"You bring me hope that my children may be alive, but they are not with me. The Great Spirit has willed it so, and seen to it that all is as it should be. Now, we must face the truth. We, the Onguiaahra tribe, are neutral, peaceful. But our brothers, the Huron, the Seneca, and the Iroquois, are not always so. We have a story to write, a great tale of war unfolding before us. It comes to us like a tide, with the changing moon, like the seasons, whether we want it or not.

"The white man advances as well," said Kohana.

Kwatoko frowned. "We must protect ourselves from the advancing front. The Huron and the Iroquois are at war. I've seen the white man assisting the Huron, living as they do. They have even given them guns, to defeat the Iroquois. But I fear them less, at this time, than our own brothers."

"You are correct. Kohana, lead a tribe of men to scope out the mighty Iroquois. Be cautious. Observe. But remain neutral for now."

"Yes, sir," said Kohana.

With his arms outstretched, Honovi faced the others. "Nihol, Kwatoko, surround and reinforce the village."

"We will do so at once, sir," said Nihol.

Nihol, Kwatoko and Kohana left the longhouse in haste.

Honovi sat alone with the cardinal, and after some time, he began to sing. He imagined Lelewala, singing back to him. Behind the falls in her new home, Lelewala had often done the same, summoning an unknown past, in the roar of the raging Niagara Falls, where her voice was drowned by its majesty, when no one heard her song of longing or wished to discover where she was from, the years lost from her story and dimmed from her life, a candle extinguished. Honovi's song promised that Lelewala and Dyani were still his children, and that a father's love was important and eternal, though they were not with him.

Dyani sang out as he wandered in the forest, too, at times, "I'm out here. I'm on my own now."

And before Honovi retired that evening, he asked in song as he stepped out of the longhouse and he gazed to the sky at a blood moon set low, unveiled and then concealed repeatedly by the swift gray cumulus of an incoming cold front, "Are you still out there? There is still hope."

His hair stood on end. He wrapped his shoulders in a bear skin cloak and the cardinal, Jaci, snuggled near his ear.

Jaci asked, "Chief, you didn't really mean what you said about giving up hope looking for Lelewala, did you?"

Honovi admitted, "Of course not. But to the tribe, I must remain strong. In my heart, my children are alive. And perhaps I was too hard on Dyani."

"Maybe Dyani needed some time in the real world to sink or swim. He's a hunter."

"A hunter. That's what I'm worried about," said Honovi.

CHAPTER 22

As the summer approached, Dyani remained a vagrant of The Land, and his appearance could not be described any more kindly, without lying, as anything better than disheveled. In fact, at times he looked derelict, with a lengthy beard that he cut from time to time, and long, snarled hair, and often a dirty face. But he was well muscled now, and he had filled out, and Frekki followed him everywhere. He had developed an outstanding eye for hunting game and an incredible timing for catching fish. The two wanderers were anything but starving now, and Dyani had put on several pounds that summer alone.

Now, as they walked among the shaded gorge, he shot and he hit a buck with a full, meaty breast and a dozen points on its antlers. Frekki shot an apple from the tree. Sallali raced toward it as it fell, and she caught it. It made a splitting sound as she bit into the ripe fruit.

"Ha-ha! Did you see that Frekki?"

"Venison stew tonight. I never thought I'd see the day," said Frekki.

"Sadly, it's feast or famine out here. When my father banished me from the village, I had to learn to hunt, or we would've starved." Dyani rubbed Sallali on the head, then he shot a bullseye on a tree he'd made for practice, hit its center precisely.

"Right on boss! Look at that shot. Even Inola would be jealous."

Dyani smiled, and then suddenly, he stopped, and he turned and he looked around. "Sometimes I can feel his spirit in me, and in these trees, and in all The Land."

"I just wish we could find Lele."

"We must keep looking. Chumana said Lelewala was near these waters, near Niagara Falls. I'll live in this gorge until we find her."

"But we can't get any closer to the rapids without angering the Thunder God, and well," Frekki whispered to Dyani, "Chumana's not exactly the most reliable source, boss."

Dyani said firmly, "Lelewala is alive. I know she is. Chumana wasn't lying. Not about this."

Frekki had a strong bite when he was angry, especially for a wolf who'd been the runt of his mother's litter, but he was often one of the gentlest creatures in the forest, and now, he said softly, as he placed his paw on Dyani's forearm, "Dyani, it's been three years. Maybe we should go back to the village and show your father how you've changed, what a skilled hunter you are. He'd want you back in the tribe right away. You could feed the whole Indian nation with your skills now."

Dyani pulled his arm away. "My father doesn't believe me. He thinks my pact with the snake maiden was real. I shouldn't have lied, not even for her crazy attempt to return to the village. I'm no better than her, and now no one would believe my word is worth anything."

"Don't be so hard on yourself." The wolf whimpered.

"You don't know my father's wrath when he's angry. I'm sure it could match Heno's."

"Let's not try and find out."

They walked along in silence, and after a while, there was a rustle in the bushes. An enormous white bear, much like the one in young Lelewala's story, was rummaging through the forest.

Though Frekki was gifted with incredible hearing and a keen sense of smell, he did not see the bear immediately, only stopped, asked, "Did you hear something?"

"I appreciate you trying to make me feel better, Frekki, but there's no one here," said Dyani. He reached above him to pick an apple, and he rubbed it on his chest, and he bit into the crisp fruit, heard its crack.

"No, I mean besides the sound of you wallowing in stubborn pride and self-pity. I thought I heard something."

Dyani turned, just as the great bear appeared from the brambles beside Frekki. He dropped the fruit and he pointed and he screamed, "Frekki, look out!"

The bear pulled back the tree and swatted a heavy paw at Frekki. Frekki moved nimbly away. The bear lunged at Dyani, knocking him over and swatting Sallali out of the way. The black squirrel climbed up the bear's oily coat and onto its head, and she covered its coal black eyes with her tiny paws. Frekki growled, baring his sharp teeth, bit the bear in the rear end, angering it further. The massive animal shook Frekki, who had all of his teeth still planted, and it hurled him forward, over the top of him.

Frekki landed on Dyani.

Dyani wrestled, rolling beneath the bear, then over it, several fierce turns in the muddy brush, until the bear pinned him, stood eleven feet tall. The ferocious beast hovered over Dyani as he cowered, and it was about to shred his flesh with pointed claws, when Dyani remembered one of Lelewala's stories.

"The soles of his feet, Frekki! Like in Lele's story. Shoot him in the soles of his feet."

Frekki took aim, pierced one of the bear's paws with his arrow.

The bear howled, trying to remove the arrow. Frekki shot another arrow into its other foot. It rolled about the ground, whimpering.

"I know the legend says that the white bear can only hunt us if we're not on his trail first, but let's not stick around to find out, boss."

Dyani grabbed a splintered piece of driftwood, swam with Frekki and Sallali on his back to the other side of the lower river.

Then Dyani looked back to the bank where the creature lay. As the great bear bled into the water, onto the rocks and onto the scales of fishes, the leaves on the trees began to fall around him, and they turned to autumn hues of yellow squash and pumpkin and a citrine yellow-green and earth-brown, and finally, a ferric red that resembled the creature's own blood.

Just as Lelewala had described.

"I don't care what anyone says. You really are a wolf, Frekki." Dyani mussed the hair on Frekki's scalp.

Frekki growled, smiling a broad grin. "I'm no fox, but I'm smart enough to know that was a close call, Dyani. We're really out on our own out here—with wild animals and the Iroquois and the Hurons at war. And the white man. Don't forget about the white man!"

Sallali's teeth chattered.

Dyani laughed. "You had me convinced at the giant white bear." Then he looked around him. Before his eyes, it seemed, it was autumn again. "Look! The leaves are changing."

"Like Lele's story. She's close. I can feel it."

"Let's eat and build a fire for the night and keep searching for her in the morning. I never said I didn't miss home, but if I go back to the village, it'll be with my sister, or it'll be when I'm dead."

CHAPTER 23

The following morning, behind Niagara Falls, Janok and Lelewala were dressed to wed. Agatha had adorned Lelewala's dark tendrils with a wreath of baby's breath, and she had made her a dress of white lace and a bouquet of lilacs and tulips and lilies, which she now held at her waist. Ava had cooked a feast fit for the Gods, for after all, they were, and Ana had made clouds shaped of moons and hearts and stars, and thrown them up to the sky especially for the occasion. Grapes from the surrounding vineyards abounded, and Heno had seen that they were harvested just after a biting frost. The syrupy wine they produced bubbled from every fountain in the cave, and had given Ava an embarrassing case of the hiccups that resembled the squawk of the largest of Amazon parrots.

The three sisters attended the ceremony as bridesmaids, while Moki was rather charming the way he smoothed his fur for the occasion. Can't you picture him in a tuxedo, ready to perform the ceremony beside Heno? As Moki stood high on the podium, Janok and Lelewala turned and faced each other. Smiling, Janok lifted Lelewala's veil. A birdsong orchestra played for them as they took their vows.

Deer and seagulls gathered, and even the fishes rose to the surface to witness the royal event, leaping high and making splashes among the rapids.

Janok's sisters swooned with teary eyes.

Heno cleared his throat. "An old Indian saying goes, we will be known forever by the family we leave. And what is life?"

Moki grew dramatic and serious, closing his eyes and pointing his nose to the sky, and he raised one paw to the heavens.

"It is but the light of a firefly to mortals. Today, my son's bride shall join the Gods in the immortal kingdom, and they shall be forever wed. Lelewala, do you take this handsome, strong, intelligent, hunk of a—"

Janok gave Heno an annoyed, impatient look of disbelief. "Dad!"

"Sorry. Sorry."

Janok whispered to his father, "Don't be weird, dad."

"Ahem. Sorry. Just so proud of you, son." Heno beamed.

"Keep going."

Moki opened a little book then, from which Heno read, "Lelewala, do you take Janok to be your husband?"

Lelewala nodded excitedly. "I do."

"And do you, my only son, take this beautiful maiden, who I single-handedly rescued from death on the rocks below the great Niagara Falls, to be your lovely wife?"

"I do, father," Janok said.

"And Lelewala, you understand that your strength and immortal life derive from your home behind the great and mighty Niagara Falls, and all its magnificent power?"

Lelewala was prepared to answer quickly, as she nodded, but at that instant, a fleeting image appeared before her: Inola dying, hitting the cold ground where he would remain, Dyani scolding her, then running off, talking to the owl, and finally, going over the falls.

She stared blankly.

"Lelewala?" said Janok.

"Are you having second thoughts, fair maiden?" asked Heno.

Lelewala focused on the ceremony again. "No, I'm not having second thoughts. I'll remain here with you always, Janok." She smiled. "I love you."

"Then you may kiss the bride," said Heno.

The daughters cheered, scattered blossoms along the rocks. Janok and Lelewala kissed a long and passionate kiss that linked their bodies from head to toe, and after what seemed an eternity, they were done, and then they stood still, regarding each other earnestly. Ava and Ana and Agatha danced around them, swinging them around, arm in arm, in a square dance of sorts. At this point, friend, imagine Moki shedding his tuxedo jacket and donning his squirrel-sized sunglasses and becoming the D.J. for the event, with two turn tables and a microphone. A laser light show illuminating the cave.

The music kicked up, and the wedding celebration ensued.

"You had me worried there, Lelewala. For a minute, I thought you'd changed your mind," said Janok.

Lelewala turned away. "I didn't change my mind. It's just that—"

"Lelewala, you can tell me." Janok took her hand.

"I'm starting to remember things. I remember going over Niagara Falls. And the snake maiden."

"That's perfect! Then you understand—the fall, the snake maiden. You're lucky to be alive."

"I am. And I'm so glad I found you, Janok. I feel like I'm telling the real life story I always wanted to, but sometimes, I feel like a ghost. Like there's still something I'm forgetting. Or someone, somewhere..."

"I can understand wanting to forget Chumana, the snake maiden. She's enough to give anyone nightmares."

CHAPTER 24

Down the river, Chumana watched the marriage ceremony in her evil whirlpool. Kangee, her trusted spy, and source of inside information, who had shared the news of the event, was perched on her shoulder. He was still sticky and covered with sweet maple syrup, and he squawked as Chumana's tongue protruded, licked him clean. Devils and demons danced about in the waters of Chumana's whirlpool. She stirred the pot with a branch. Its green glow reflected on her skin.

"Can you believe this, Kangee? The snot nosed maiden married to the son of a God? And what do I have—nothing!"

"She will tell great *ssstories* once again now that she *remembersss* who she is." The raven hissed.

"Shut up. Don't remind me. We can't let that happen. I'll be the greatest storyteller of The Land yet. Even The Great Spirit will hear what I have to say." Chumana rubbed the scales that were starting to blossom from her skin. They flaked off in airy crusts. Thinking, she said, "We have to get rid of Honovi. It's going to be harder than I thought."

"With power comes much *resssponsibility*..."

"That's right!" She flung Kangee into the whirlpool and he flew out, squawking and preening himself. "And I'll be responsible for all the tribes of the Indian Nations. I'll rule The Land with my words. I have to come up with a plan."

Kangee said, "Lelewala can no longer return to the village. Her terrible fall took all of her strength. Poor girl. But Heno made her a potion."

"That's it! What I need is a potion. I'm not talking about a veggie smoothie or a love potion. I need a little poison! Not only poison in my words, but poison in the water."

Now Chumana sang a mystical song of poison. She dug up a salamander, maroon and covered in earth. She licked it with her black tongue and bit its tail and popped the rest into her mouth. Then she opened a jar of earthworms and shook them out of the jar and down her throat and she expelled a loud belch.

"You're a nervous eater," Kangee said. "Next time, save some for me."

"Let's go, Kangee. We'll use the war between the tribes to poison the minds of the chiefs, you *ssseee*. A few white lies can manipulate *hissstory*, bend it to one's own will. And nothing controls the *massses* more than fear!"

Chumana finished her snack, started through the forest. She transformed herself into human form, hiding her face and her tongue with a cape of purple velvet.

"Look ahead, Kangee. It's the Seneca Chief, Annenraes."

The warrior, Chief Annenraes, approached, wearing a headdress. "Who goes there?"

"What is the *ssstrongest* Indian chief in all The Land doing out alone today? Are the mighty Senecas not at war with the Huron?" Chumana was coy. She circled slyly around the chief and smiled with her almond eyes, hiding her tongue.

"It's true. And what tribe do you belong to, maiden? And why do you hide your face?"

"I'm but one of the neutrals, lost from my village." Chumana pulled her scarf up further. Kangee's tongue appeared from his long beak. The bird was sitting on her shoulder. Glaring sideways, she shot him a look of warning.

Annenraes pointed off in the distance. "The Onguiaahra village is back that way. It is dangerous to proceed in this direction. Beyond this stream, the Indian nations battle. Great bloodshed may taint thy eyes if you proceed any further, maiden."

Chumana pulled a vial from her cloak. "Thank you for warning me. Please accept this drink to quench your weary thirst. It is a gift of my *thanksss*."

"You are gracious, kind maiden." The chief drank the potion down in one gulp. "I thank you. You must return to your village now. I will soon order my men to advance in this direction. Take safety. Follow the river home."

"Thank you, brave warrior. I will do so at once."

Chumana waved goodbye now and with an evil smile, she looked over her shoulder and she licked her lips and she pulled down her scarf and she turned around. Chief Annenraes had already collapsed to the ground.

"It worked. That potion will make him sleep for days."

"The Seneca chief *asssleep* from your poison," said Kangee.

Chumana stroked Kangee's head. "Yes, *asssleep*. He's dead to the whole world. But it's Chief Honovi I'm after. Let's go! We've got a bigger fish to catch."

Kangee squawked. "*Sssomeone* is coming."

"Hurry, to the river." Chumana transformed behind a cloud of yellow smoke, morphing into snake form, and she pierced the water in a jack knife dive, swimming upstream toward the falls.

Behind her, the Indian tribe came up close behind, searching for their Chief Annenraes, who lay face down now, in a pile of molded leaves.

CHAPTER 25

Dyani, Frekki and Sallali crept up the walls of the Niagara gorge, twice skidding downward in a muddy landslide of debris and rocks caused by the Jogahs and Gagongas. Dyani crawled upward through the dogwood and white birch and spruce that grew like ropey fingers of giants from the walls of the rock and ledges of sediment in all their unique layers. They'd heard the beautiful music and gentle voices of the sisters that carried throughout the forest as if it had flown with grace on the wings of hummingbirds. The mystical sounds and the smell of baked apples and honey in the crisp air now led them, spellbound, closer to Niagara Falls. When they were close, Frekki pointed to the sky, at the oddly shaped clouds that Heno's daughter, Ava, had created.

Dyani sighted the wedding party. "Look, down there!"

Frekki's head was still in the clouds, so to speak, and he was only half listening to Dyani, when he said, "Is it the white man? The Senecas? The Iroquois! Let me at 'em. I can take 'em."

"Whiteman?" Dyani grimaced, and he crept stealthily prone, hiding in the sumac. "Easy, Frekki." He parted the leaves and he wrinkled his nose and he remarked, "It's a bunch of...girls dancing."

"Girls? Mademoiselles?" Frekki perked up and scrambled over top of Dyani through the brush, blocking his line of sight to the gathering below.

Dyani shooed him out of the way, leaned in closer. Then an echo deafened their speech.

Dyani covered his ears. "The echo. It's so loud. Almost like thunder."

Sallali nodded, scurrying up onto Dyani's shoulder, making roaring pantomimes and pointing down at the entrance to the cave of the winds. Imagine the little squirrel dressed in a yellow rain coat and holding an umbrella as the wind blew at her and the rain pelted her sideways from the mist of Niagara Falls. At once, Dyani knew what she meant.

"That's it. Isn't it? It's the Cave of the Winds. Right down there." Dyani jumped up and he scooped up Sallali and kissed her. "The home of Heno, the thunder God!"

Sallali nodded excitedly, pointing.

"I've got to get down there," Dyani said.

Frekki warned, "Be careful. The rocks are dangerous. They're slippery and wet and..."

But Dyani had already started down the treacherous path.

Frekki had allowed his excitement to get the best of him, and he slipped now, slobbering and bumping all the way down the primitive rock stairway which was covered in a coating of moss and fractals of mushroom bunches and a carpet of lichens. Dyani skillfully navigated his way to the bottom. Sallali slid down it after them as if it were a lofty water slide, and she bumped into Frekki and she knocked him forward onto all fours. Before Frekki could scold little Sallali, they were taken by what they saw next.

Dyani beheld Lelewala, staring off alone on the rocks. She was petting Moki, while three maidens laughed and danced, not far from her.

The young maidens spotted them at once, and before Dyani could protest, Ava took his arm. Then Ana pulled him in the opposite direction. Soon, all three of the sisters were fighting over who would be the first to dance with him. Dyani went along, keeping Lelewala in his line of sight, as the sisters spun him into a dizzying round of do-si-do, square dancing about the slippery rocks.

Ada called, "Lelewala, come dance! Janok's making thunder with Papa. Don't be scared. We do this all the time down here."

Lelewala laughed, and she rubbed Moki's head. "We need to find you a companion Moki."

Moki pointed to Sallali.

Ada skipped across the rock bridge where Lelewala stood now, pulled her across playfully, towards them. Heno's thunder made a celebratory crack overhead, and she looked to the sky, startled. She was still looking up—these sights and sounds and festivities were completely novel to her—when Ada pulled her faster, whisking her into the dancing circle. As Dyani do-si-do'ed away from Agatha, Lelewala and Dyani smacked into each other abruptly. By this time, both Dyani and Lelewala were vertiginous, and their feet wobbled like wooden marionettes. Finally, they steadied themselves.

"Excuse me," said Dyani.

Lelewala said, "I'm so sorry, I—"

Lelewala and Dyani stopped to stare at each other for a moment now. While Lelewala had been piecing together her memory, lapses still remained. Dyani was the first to speak.

"Lelewala," he said.

"It's nice to meet you—"

"Dyani. It's Dyani," he said.

To Ada, Lelewala whispered, "Is he part of the family?"

Ada said, "He's not from our side."

Ava was enamored. "He's so handsome. If he's a wedding crasher, he can stay."

Agatha wasn't giving up a chance with the handsome Dyani so easily, though, and she pulled him away from Lelewala, and she blurted, "I saw him first. He's my *'and guest,'* for the reception."

To Ava and Ada, Lelewala remarked, "I'm not sure who he is but..." She traced the outline of Dyani's face as he moved away from her with Agatha, and then she touched her own, and she said, "he resembles me."

The song ended and another began, this one slower. Her orchestra was the delicate Bridal Veil Falls beside her, the birdsongs of the gulls and sparrows and jays and cardinals, and Lelewala felt a musical story brewing within her somehow, but she listened and watched as the mysterious guest danced with her sister in-law. Lelewala sang her own words. "Something about him is familiar."

Dyani sang back. "Remember. Remember where you've come from and what led you here. I came to help you, please don't fear. Sister, I'm sorry."

Lelewala's voice strengthened then, and her lyrics were, "I've learned myself, and I've been told, what story awaits, what history unfolds."

Dyani and Lelewala sang back and forth and, after some time, their identities became clear. She realized then that she was singing to her brother. He was the warrior in her visions, the one who had shot and killed the great hunter. They faced each other now, and they hugged.

Janok entered the room, misunderstood the embrace. "Lelewala, is this what you meant about someone else? You were in love with someone else before you fell over the falls?"

"Janok, no! He's my brother."

Janok was relieved, sighed. "Well why didn't you say so?"

"I wasn't sure then, but I remember now. I remember everything."

CHAPTER 26

With Kangee flying beside her, Chumana swam up beside the falls, leaving in her wake a putrid odor of rotted leaves and mushrooms and the dead fish of the lower river who had fallen to their demise. As she glared at Dyani and Lelewala and Janok, she looked as disgusted as the animals she passed, who cringed as they caught a whiff of her scent.

"He found her! I can't stand it any longer, Kangee. Will you look at this mushy-gushy family moment? Not only does she have a hunk of a husband who's the son of a God, but now she's got her loving brother back."

The raven reminded her, "Her *ssstrength* is limited to the great Niagara Falls. Beyond the *fallsss*, she is weak."

"That's it. We've got to work quickly—get her away from Niagara Falls. The Niagara or Onguiaahra tribe—whatever they're called—derive their strength from it, too. They're no match for the Senecas. The Huron. I can destroy her and Chief Honovi once and for all. Otherwise, once her daddy realizes she's still alive, she'll be telling her stories again in no time, and I'll be reduced to an old maid. No one will want to listen to me."

"Or marry you..."

"Shut up!" Chumana closed Kangee's beak with her tongue in a vice-like grip. After he struggled a while, she released him, leaving him gasping for breath. Black feathers molted to the ground. "You're right, though. It doesn't matter if she can't leave Niagara Falls. They'll all come from far and wide to listen to her—she has a gift. Then no one will want to listen to me and I'll be..." she gasped, "forgotten. That's worse than being banished. I've got to work fast."

Chumana crawled out of the water, primordial in habitus, like some primitive sloth of middle earth. Legs evolved instantly from her body. She now wore a gown of green sea moss with spider web veiled over her bare shoulders, where dewdrops sparkled on her fair skin and her black hair fell lustrous in the sunlight. She approached Dyani. "Oh lover boy, didn't your invitation say, "Dyani *and guest?*"

Dyani turned. "Chumana."

"That's right, sugar poopsie. I hope your sister got a bigger rock than I did, cheapskate." From Chumana's cupids bow lips sprang her black tongue, elongated and covered in boils and tentacles and zebra mussels. She extended it out in long coils, attempting to wrap and capture Lelewala, who now screamed. Frekki cut off the end of her leathery appendage with his sword, and the tendrils encircling the bride fell to the rocks. Chumana howled, and the stump of her tongue retracted into her pursed lips.

"What's she talking about, Dyani? She's the reason I went over Niagara Falls and I almost died, not you. She convinced me it was my destiny, my story to tell."

Dyani started to explain. "Lelewala, I blamed you for Inola's death, but it wasn't your fault. The creatures of The Land wanted to hear your story—you have a special gift that no one else has. It's magical, like the God's. You belong here—with them."

Heno walked past his daughters, who were drinking and toasting cocktails of apple juice and lemon and plum, and he came out into the sunlight now where the newlyweds stood, for he'd been watching Chumana closely from the shadows. He placed his arms around Janok and Lelewala, and he said, "It's true, my children—all dreams spin from the same web. This is your home now, Lelewala." Then his expression grew menacing, and to Chumana, he said, "You snake maiden, get out of here, or I'll fry you like an eel."

Heno wrenched a lightning bolt from his belt and he threw it at Chumana's feet, where she stood with the raven in a pool of water. The water turned at once to vapors of steam, and it charred the stone beneath it and electrified the water beside her to a black sludge. Kangee alighted with a purple glow, molted his raggedy plumage in clumps of gray ash.

"I simply wanted to wish my sister in law good luck," said Chumana.

Lelewala's patience for the unknown was wearing thin now, and she said, "Sister in law? I'm looking to the left and to the right, sister, because I thought Janok and I were the ones who got married. Which one of you is she talking about?"

"Read the scroll and weep. You and I are related by blood, princess—your brother's blood. He signed it himself right here on the bottom line." Chumana unraveled the scroll with Dyani's signature.

Heno threw another spear of lightning.

Chumana disappeared behind a cloud of smoke. She transformed into snake form and jumped into the water and started to swim away, dodging Heno's display of power.

"Be gone, snake maiden," Heno called.

Dyani took Lelewala's hand, and said, "I only did it to find you, Lele. To bring you home safely. But now you're here, and father's banished me from the village for telling a lie."

Lelewala pulled away, toward Janok. "Dyani, I want to believe you. But Chumana tricked me once. How do I know you're real? I lost my memory once. I didn't know who I was, or where I came from." She ran off into the caves, crying, and she disappeared out of sight.

"Anyone who upsets Lelewala, upsets me." Janok was furious, and he roared, a spectacular roar, louder than he ever had.

"Son, I—I've never heard you roar like that before. You're starting to sound like your old man. I must say." Heno was proud, and he hugged Janok, but his son would not rest.

Speaking to Dyani and Chumana, Janok demanded, "How dare you both upset my bride on our wedding day?"

His voice did not crack.

But Chumana was swimming out of sight.

Dyani was apologetic. "I'm sorry, your highness. I—please, tell my sister to take all the time she needs. I'm just so glad she's safe. And I'm sorry for all I've said and done."

"I'm sorry. You must go," Janok said.

Dyani, saddened, turned to leave, and he said nothing more.

Janok added, "Tell that reptilian wife of yours to crawl back under whatever rock she came from."

Dyani turned. "She's not really my wife. I—I lied."

Heno asked, "Then how can you be trusted, young man? Whatever she is—she'd better watch her spineless back. I'm watching her every move."

CHAPTER 27

Night fell upon the Niagara Gorge, and the screeching of owls and rummaging of Chumana's evil raccoons and other nocturnal creatures covered in armor and not yet named by man broke the silence of the darkest hour. Kangee flew low over the rapids where Chumana's whirlpool, illuminated by only a harvest moon sullied with streaks of fog, spun violently in whorls of brown froth and murk. She stood cloaked and hooded on the riverbank in moonlight yellowed by the shadows of the immense gorge where arthropods and mollusks lay preserved, their tiny imprints withstanding the physical force of millions of years of duress and the awe-inspiring forces of massive glaciers moving west, tearing with them all things living and inorganic in their paths.

"I've got work to do, Kangee, this way! Hurry! While my sleeping poison is still working on Chief Annenraes."

Beyond them, a gathering of Senecas assembled in the forest. Chumana ran toward them. She pitched herself on the ground and called for help until one of the warriors turned and he came to her and he knelt at her side.

"What ails you, maiden?" asked the Seneca. "It's after dusk."

Chumana wept, hiding her tongue, her coiled lips. "The Onguiaahra—the neutral tribe, has taken the Indian Chief Annenraes and killed him."

"Killed him?"

Another warrior said, "Chief Annenraes is missing. Young woman, how do you know he's dead?"

The first, who was taller and leaner and more muscular, rose to stand, and he helped Chumana to her feet. "Are you sure it is the work of the Onguiaahra tribe?"

"I'm *csssertain*." Chumana's smile, which she kept hidden beneath her cloak, was sly. "The killers went that way—home toward their neutral village."

The second Indian addressed the group of ten. "Men, we are at war with the Huron, but it seems the neutral tribe, the peaceful Onguiaahra, are not so peace loving. We must advance at once toward their village. They've killed our chief!"

By the moonlight, the others called, "Attack!"

Chumana uncovered her head, and she stroked Kangee's feathers, smiled, and she watched the Indians charge on toward the neutral village, the tribe of Chief Honovi.

The sun had slipped beneath the horizon, and slowly, every streak of crimson disappeared from the sky, and blurred to a violet and then to a dark void, where stars radiated, came together in constellations and asterisms, smaller star patterns within the constellations. Giant pictures of Canes Venatici, the hunting dogs, Orion, the hunter, and the largest, Hydra, the water snake, popped, one by one, against the lightless midnight backdrop.

Outside the longhouses where women and children slept on planks of knotted maple, the tribal council assembled fireside. An owl called out and flew from its nest. From the forest to the east of their village on the Niagara peninsula came the sound of feet, pounding on the hardened ground, a steady crescendo.

Chief Honovi, who had been speaking, stopped, listened. The council was silent. The owl screeched again.

The trampling sounds intensified.

A dozen men. A hundred maybe. It was impossible to tell. War cries now. Great yelps calling for revenge of those wronged. The sounds could not be mistaken for anything other than a call to war. A surprise attack. Honovi's men were not prepared for such a game. He sent Kwatoko to the perimeter of the village.

Kwatoko ran out, returned quickly.

"They have another war to fight with the Huron. What has prompted such a surprise and sudden attack on our tribe? We have done nothing to anger them." Honovi and his men armed themselves.

Further in the village, the others were awakening and wandering, purgatoid, toward the exterior of their homes.

"They claim we have taken their chief, Annenraes," said Kwatoko. "They're calling for a swift and bloody end to our tribe."

"We have not. There is only one who would spread such lies. We have maintained a neutral position, done no harm to others."

Nihol said, "Chumana."

Honovi frowned. "Yes, I have been too lenient. That beast will stop at nothing until she destroys this village. She must be stopped, and killed."

"There is no reasoning with the Huron now. We are at war," said Nihol.

Honovi took his bow, and he sharpened several arrows and he secured them in the papoose on his back. Then he spit into the fire. "You are right. Although it is not our way, we must fight now. Find their chief at once. It is not the Onguiaahra who have taken him. Whoever rights this wrong will be honored to serve on the tribal council for life."

Kwatoko said, "I will gather a search party and organize an army."

Honovi said, "Jaci, fly far and wide, over all The Land. Search and find the Seneca Chief Annenraes. If anyone has seen or heard from him, I must be notified at once."

"Yes, your Chiefliness."

"And Jaci?"

The little cardinal preened his feathers, gave a salute. "Yes, sir?"

"I'll handle the snake maiden myself."

CHAPTER 28

After the last wine-soaked sesame-crusted bread sticks and chocolate-dolloped custard cream puffs had been eaten, and after the last round of karaoke had been sung, Heno made a final, thundering roar. Then, being as pleased as he had been in a very long time, he retired for the evening. Moki was licking his paws after finishing a delicious snack of fries and cheese curds covered generously in gravy. The sisters were in a drunken state of livelihood and giddy with excitement, and while they very much wished that their brother hadn't scared off the handsome guest, Dyani, they were caught up in memories of their childhood, and did not allow it to affect their happy go lucky evening. Eventually, though, they stumbled off to bed, with boisterous laughing interspersed with a hiccup or two. They found their way into a pleasant lull, dreaming of how they'd convince their father to allow them, like Janok, to marry, and seek the company of the outside world. It seemed a satisfying end to the day.

Lelewala, however, anxiously paced behind the falls.

"Lelewala, I underestimated you. You scored yourself a real hunk," said Frekki.

Moki nodded.

"I underestimated you, too, Frekki. You were so brave. You helped Dyani find me here." Lelewala shook her head. "I just don't know what to believe."

"I don't like to shake my own tail, but you should've seen me when the bear came after Dyani. I gave him one of these," Frekki said, and he punched the air. "Then I showed him these." He growled, bared his teeth.

"The bear? The great white bear of legends?"

"You got it. Gristly teeth. Big, hairless body."

Lelewala said, "Then the legend is true. My storytelling serves a real purpose. My people need me. To pass on the words and history of our past."

"You better believe it, princess."

"Dyani really did risk his life to find me then..."

"Yep. And that deal he made with the snake maiden, we can get that fixed," said Frekki.

Lelewala wasn't convinced. "But I saw the marriage scroll. It was signed in his own blood."

"There must be a way to—"

Lelewala stopped. "I have to see my father again. To warn him of Chumana's intentions to destroy him, and the village, with her lies."

"But Lele, from what your hubby was sayin', your strength only lasts as long as you're by the falls." Frekki was worried. "It's a miracle you're even alive."

"I put the lives of everyone in the village at risk when I left. I must make it right. Tonight, I'll stay here with my husband. But tomorrow, I will tell Heno that I must go out to warm my father. If I'm not strong enough to return, so be it."

Frekki protested, staring at Lelewala through the mist. "But Lele—"

Janok's voice echoed loudly as he entered the room. "Lelewala? Are you all right?"

"Yes, Janok, I'm fine. I'm here," she said.

Janok hugged her. "I was worried about you. Please don't ever leave me. You have no idea what it was like here without you. You've brought life to this place. Even my father and sisters are different with you here. I need you. And I'll protect you here, keep you strong."

Lelewala hugged Janok and she kissed him, but her thoughts raced with what she knew she had to accomplish. If there was a way, any way at all, that she could warn her father and her tribe of their impending doom without hurting Janok, she would, of course, do it, but at that moment, she decided that the safety of her people was more important than her own happiness—maybe even her own life.

CHAPTER 29

The following morning, Lelewala awoke before anyone else in the Cave of the Winds. Moki was next to open his eyes, and he followed Lelewala as she sneaked past the three sisters' bedrooms. The girls were soundly sleeping. Ada's hair was in rollers and Agatha was drooling with her mouth open, and Ana, why, Lelewala had never heard such sonorous noise before—and from the mouth of a princess—Ana's snoring could be heard down the hall. Lelewala stopped a minute at her door, for she thought Ana was stirring, and that she would awaken and ask her where she was going, but Ana went back to sleep, and Lelewala shrugged, and she thought that, after all, Ana *was* the daughter of a thunder maker. Ana's little rumbles of thunder shook the caves, vibrating the stalactites and layers of slate in the ceiling and walls. Lelewala waited a moment at her doorway, then crept past it, and proceeded tiptoe down the hall.

She had just turned the corner, when she ran smack into Heno.

"Oh, excuse me, Heno, great God of Thunder."

Heno was still waking up. He stretched and yawned and ushered Lelewala into the kitchen where the sun shone through the rock caves in prisms of intense light, through quartz and crystalline walls, and he made Lelewala some coffee. "Please, uh, call me dad."

"Dad, I—"

He was making pancakes now and breaking eggs, whipping them up with a whisk. He turned back where Lelewala was seated at the massive granite table. "I like to start the day right. Maybe a little apple juice, an omelet."

"I need to ask you a favor."

"Anything for my daughter in law. We're family now. And especially if it means I might get some grandchildren—little thunder makers—I can hear the pitter-patter now." Heno flipped his omelet.

"I need to leave Niagara Falls," said Lelewala.

Heno dropped and broke an egg on the floor, and with it, he looked as though his eyeballs had fallen out and rolled around on the floor beside it. "Anything but that!"

Lelewala tried to explain. "Not forever, just today. I love Janok. I promise to return."

Heno sat down beside Lelewala, and he said, "Lelewala, I saved you from your doom when I rescued you, but what you don't know is—I cast a spell on you so that your strength would only fare behind the falls. Janok was lonely, he was going to leave me, and—"

"You used me to make him stay? So you tricked me." She thought she was the one who needed to explain, apologize, even, but with Heno's sudden confession, a look of betrayal spread across her face.

"Not exactly, I—"

"I'm going either way. Chumana is poisoning The Land with her lies, and she intends to harm my people—and my father. I must warm them at least, even if I fall down weak, and die."

Heno protested. "There's no telling how you'll fare out there. And against the snake maiden? You'll be no match."

"Father, I love Janok. I want to return to him, but not at the risk of losing my entire village. My foolishness has caused enough problems." Lelewala was sorrowful.

She turned to leave.

Heno grumbled, and said, "Wait, daughter. Your story is virtuous and true. You love my son. He's never been happier. Even my daughters are thrilled. I'll make you a potion that will give you enough strength for one day. But you must return before sunset."

Lelewala jumped up, and she spun around and then she grabbed Heno's hand and took it and she hugged him and kissed him on the cheek. "Oh, Heno—Dad, I mean. Thank you! Thank you!"

When Lelewala set out that morning, a frost had just lifted from the ground, and her feet froze in her moccasins as they trampled crisp leaves fallen from the birch trees, etched black like a beast had clawed their design upon their trunks with daggered nails. Moki and Frekki followed her, quickly, along the footpath where roads diverged many times, twisting, toward the hidden neutral village. After an hour or so, Lelewala reached a portion of the trail that followed the steady course of the Niagara, far upstream where across the river was a vast island rather shaped like a large pork chop.

"Hurry, Frekki. We must warn my father," Lelewala said.

She carried Moki under her arm, where the little squirrel struggled to keep warm, and she had only set him down for a moment when Chumana swam up beside her near the riverbank.

Kangee, looking ravenous at what looked like a delicious meal, swooped down and scooped up Moki in his pointed beak and flew up and above the waters.

At once, Lelewala turned.

Chumana floated closer to the riverbank. She cackled and coughed up thick chunks of algae, and she wound them around her serpentine tongue. Then she swallowed the regurgitated plant and expelled a large belch.

"You're a bit far from home, aren't you, fair maid of the *missst*?" She laughed haughtily, mocking Heno.

Kangee made low fly-bys over Frekki's head, taunting him with the squirrel. Frekki and Lelewala jumped, grasping toward the sky, at the hovering bird, and at Moki, who Kangee now held suspended from his claws.

"Let him go, Chumana," shouted Lelewala.

Chumana licked the slime from her lips and retracted her black tongue into her mouth. "If you've come to warn your father, it's too late. The Seneca believe he killed their chief, and they're busy destroying your pathetic neutral tribe for it. The Onguiaahra are weak and unprepared for war. They don't stand a chance."

"My father would never kill another chief—that's a cowardly act—a plan only you would concoct," Lelewala said.

Kangee made another swoop, this time flying lower. Lelewala jumped higher, grasping to reach Moki. Kangee rose with wings askew, climbing higher into the forest until suddenly, he was shot abreast with the point of an arrow, parabolic in its course and aimed precisely at its moving target. Dyani had entered the clearing and shot Kangee with exact timing. Moki now fell to the ground, claws outstretched with his tail erect and his brown hair spiked on end. Dyani's companion, Sallali, ran beneath Moki as he fell. He caught him with outstretched paws, and the black squirrel was at once, love struck.

Chumana raced to catch Kangee, but her beloved pet was dead, as stiff as a board, with his eyes bulging from their sockets and his beak, open, in a rictus of desperation. The raven bled from the wound, and his feathers wilted, flaccid quills sparsely covering his body, revealing crepes of tan flesh where they grew.

"Kangee, no," cried Chumana.

Lelewala turned. "Dyani?"

"Lele, please believe me. I should never have made that pact with Chumana. Telling lies only made things worse."

"I believe you. I never knew you could hunt. You couldn't shoot the back of a longhouse before," said Lelewala.

"I've learned a few things out here on my own." Dyani laughed.

"I hate to interrupt your family reunion, but you'll have to get by more than the mighty Senecas." Chumana began to stir up the water of the upper Niagara. Devils and spirits flew from it now, and the sky that was golden with rays of sunlight grew dark around her.

Lelewala stumbled, fell to the ground, and when she got up, she straightened her frame, and she said, "Dyani, I'm already feeling weak. I have to get back to the falls, or I'll die. You must warm father about the snake maiden."

Chumana's lower body swelled. She laughed from the bottom of her stomach, and she unscrewed the top from a vial of red poison and she swirled it around and she poured it into the flowing Niagara. The river alighted and bubbled with the stench of rotting corpses. Steam rose up through the cracks of rocks like some ancient fjord, and the river that once coursed steadily and clear looked now, more like a hell fire.

"It's too late," said Chumana, laughing. "One sip from the river and even the strongest warrior chief will die."

Frekki, who could no longer stand it, raced up and jumped in the river and swam over to the snake maiden. With his teeth gleaming, he bit Chumana on the tail, drawing blood. She flung him off with ease, but her tail oozed blood into the water.

"*Haha!* More poison." She laughed. "How cute. The little fox wants to defend Princess Lelewala and her brother. Maybe you'd like a drink. You look thirsty." Chumana coiled her tail around Frekki, and she turned him upside down and forced his snout close to the water.

Frekki spit a mouthful of the red water directly in her face. "I'm a wolf, you creepy old witch. And you might be a snake, but you've got dragon breath." Frekki cringed, turning his face away from Chumana's head and mouth as she now breathed fire from it.

"Frekki!" called Lelewala. She stumbled again, reaching out in vain, but this time she couldn't get up.

Frekki broke loose, and he swam from the river and ran to the shore, rushing to Lelewala's side. "Come on, Lele! You can do it. We have to warn the village."

Dyani said, "I'll hold off the snake maiden. Tell father and the others at once of her poison. He won't listen to me."

With Frekki helping her along, Lelewala limped toward the village. They hadn't gone far from the riverbank when they came upon an Indian chief, yawning and stretching as though he had just awakened from hibernation. His headdress was rumpled, with feathers missing. His clothes were wrinkled.

"Stop! Who goes before the princess?" asked Frekki.

The Indian said, "It is I, Annenraes, the Seneca chief."

"Your men are attacking our village—the neutral Onguiaahra tribe," said Lelewala. Even her voice was weak now, and she pleaded with him breathlessly. "I beg you. Please call off the attack."

Annenraes waved her off, and he stretched, yawned again. He looked well rested, with sleep crusted in his eyes that he now rubbed away. He shrugged, smiled, and after some time, he spoke. "I never ordered an attack. I walked alone in the forest, searching out the Hurons. A beautiful woman gave me a drink, and I fell asleep under a large oak tree. Why, I feel like I've slept one hundred years! I feel like a teenager." With this, he jumped onto a ledge of rock and squatted and set his arms out in the air as if he were surfing an ocean wave never known to him, with great vitality and purpose.

Perhaps they had expected more from the leader of the Senecas, for Lelewala and Frekki looked at each other just then like they didn't know where to begin.

Frekki said, "Look, we'll fill you in on the details later, big guy. The snake maiden made you fall asleep—she put a spell on you and told the tribes that the neutrals killed you. They think you're dead."

"She's poisoned the water in the villages so she can get revenge on my father, and tell her stories. She wants everyone to fear her—it's the only way they'll listen to her black tongued lies. Otherwise, she has no influence over anyone."

Annenraes looked confused, and he spat and he scratched his chin. "But..."

Frekki saw that Lelewala's strength was almost gone—she stumbled again.

With a worried look, she said, "There's no time to explain, you must help me find my father and call off the attack."

"The story you tell of adventure intrigues me, young lady, but do you swear it is the truth?" said Annenraes.

Before Lelewala could convince the Seneca leader, who was still, at this time, only half awake from his slumber, her father, Chief Honovi, entered the clearing. He was adorned in full war paint, and preceded by several of the fiercest warriors of his tribe, who stood poised to attack Annenraes.

Honovi said, "My daughter speaks the truth. She never lies."

"Father!" Lelewala ran to him, stumbling.

"My daughter is alive!" Honovi embraced her.

"Father, there's no time to explain. I'm weak," she said. "I must get back to Niagara Falls, or my strength will give out. I came to warn you of Chumana's poison. Tell no one to drink the water. It's filled with her venom."

"We must stop her for good this time. I've waited long enough to put an end to her mischief."

Frekki asked, "What about the Senecas?"

Annenraes said, "I'll call off the attack at once, and wage war against her. Together, we'll stop her."

Above them, the sky blackened, consumed by the flanking line of an electrical storm moving from the southwest, off the lower lake. Clouds pitched sideways, flattening as they spun into vacuous funnels. Chumana thrashed about the water, dodging arrows from Frekki and Dyani. Lelewala cringed as a bolt of lightning splintered a tree only yards from her.

"Oh father. That's a warning from Heno. I'm certain of it. I must get back before sun down."

"Oh?" Honovi asked.

Lelewala explained. "Heno granted me just enough strength to warn you of danger—of Chumana's poison in the water. I'm growing weak, father, and I must return to my home by sunset."

"Your home is here, daughter."

"There's much I need to say, but there's little time, father."

Honovi nodded as if he understand, but sorrow covered his face. His eyes had aged beyond their years in the time that Lelewala had been missing, and in the wrinkled pits beneath his eyes, his tears pooled. Without her stories, her influence on him, Honovi had lost his passion for life, even for leadership.

Honovi said, "Frekki, Jaci. Tell my men to advance towards the falls at once. I will take you to the Thunder God, daughter."

Honovi carried a canoe through the trampled footpath of goldenrod and Queen Ann's lace and dried purple thistle, all the way to the river, and he lifted Lelewala and he set her in the canoe and they advanced downstream where Dyani and Frekki battled the snake maiden.

At the same time, Annenraes' tribe of Seneca warriors charged toward the river.

Honovi paddled swiftly, steering the canoe between boulders worn smooth by rapids fierce and unrelenting, between islands broken off of the larger land mass and set adrift on their own fate of erosion and weathering. Whitecaps broke and splashed into the boat, and Honovi steadied it beside the bank, and he approached Chumana.

"I've poisoned the water. Your men will soon die, Honovi. Then I'll control all The Land. The nations will listen to all I have to say." Chumana cackled.

Honovi glared at her. His voice was wrathful. "A smart leader has responsibility, not power, snake maiden. Chief Annenraes is alive, and the war between the Senecas and the neutrals is over. The only thing left to do is for me to fulfill my promise to kill you. You will never interfere with my family or the safety of my people again."

Honovi drew an arrow and he shot it at Chumana, but she batted it away with her huge tail. She manipulated the end of her tail, and she swirled the waters, and Honovi rose into a waterspout above them, from which he couldn't escape. As it spun faster, Chumana laughed, and Honovi hovered, swirling in a funnel of wind and water filled with poison. Lelewala was weakening, gasping for breath. She reached out to grab her father.

"Father, take my hand!" she called.

But Honovi spun faster as the sun set, locked in the swirling waterspout.

CHAPTER 30

Across the river, Annenraes' warriors charged forward. Steam billowed from the water, sizzling, as Chumana's tail cut through the current, creating ten foot waves that rose up and crashed on The Land and doused the advancing front of Senecas. They drew their bows taut. Dozens of arrows sprang up in elliptical paths toward Chumana, who grew up above the water so large now that she could see great lakes both west and east of the Niagara. Her brunette locks now transformed to snakes that spit and hissed venom at the Indians below, and sprang out in all directions from her head, nearly reaching the ceiling of clouds that rotated low above the water.

Jaci flew up to Chumana's face, drilled his beak at her eyes with the frequency of a woodpecker, hammering, but she batted him away. Frekki grasped at Honovi were he hovered, trapped by Chumana's spell.

Downstream, the mist of water vapor and sediments that rose from the falls could be seen for miles. Tons of this particulate energy glowed brightly against the pink sky, and the image of Heno appeared in it at that time, and it blurred from a wavy mirage into a clear picture of his face. His voice boomed with the power of one thousand horses, and he said to Lelewala that the sun was setting, and that her fate rested on her safe return, and he said that his potion was wearing off and that he had no other way to help her if she was not beside the falls.

Lelewala said, "I'm trying. Please, help warn the tribe of Chumana's poison. It floods the waters of the Niagara."

Honovi leaned forward against the spinning funnel, but he remained trapped, and it spun faster, and he struggled to breathe, as he called out, "Please, great Heno. Warn my people, the Senecas, and the Hurons, too, not to drink of the water, no matter how thirsty in battle they become. With her black tongue, Chumana has poisoned our precious resource."

Heno nodded and chanted a low pitched hum that rippled the river in standing waves, and he pointed his fingers at the clouds, and they closed in over the water and they twisted counterclockwise in violent eddies that merged into a single circulating concussion of wind, from which a twister emerged. It split into two spouts that extended up as far as the eye could see, fingers of the gods that revolved toward Chumana, as Heno chanted, "Men and Women of The Land. Let no one drink of the water of the Niagara."

On the battlefront, Annenraes said, "Seneca warriors, here is the real enemy. Defeat this beast!"

The Senecas charged at Chumana, trampling through fields of calendulas and African daisies and pale coneflowers, steadfast, toward the riverbank. They carried their canoes over their heads and set them in the water, and they paddled forth fearlessly toward the giant serpent and they hacked at her tail with tomahawks and sickled knives, and they pierced it with their arrows, but Chumana's tail swelled, and she grew larger.

Chumana lifted her tail, heaved it up, and she brought it down crashing across the river, obstructing all flow of water, backing it up for miles. The impact of this massive appendage caused a monstrous tidal wave that threw the Seneca and neutral warriors from the river, capsizing their canoes.

Heno created a thunderstorm around Chumana now that sent jagged bolts of electricity at her, lit up the water for miles. Dyani steadied his canoe and took aim at her with his bow and arrow, but he was tossed left and right in the great flood.

Dyani called, "Father, I've almost got a shot at her, just a little to the left and—"

Thunder rumbled, shaking the entire ground.

Lelewala struggled to stay upright in her canoe beside Honovi, still trapped in the water spout. She said, "Father, I'm growing weaker. I must get back to Niagara Falls, to my home, and to my husband, Janok."

"Husband?" Honovi said. "Lelewala, not again. You'll drown. It's a trick."

Dyani said, "It's true, father. She's the bride to Heno's son, Janok. Her marriage is real. Mine was a lie that caused these problems."

Frekki steadied Lelewala's canoe, and he shouted, "It's confusing, but try to keep up, your Chiefliness. We'll bring you up to speed later."

Chumana released her tail where it obstructed the river, and the dammed water caused a flood of incredible magnitude that washed Lelewala downstream, away from Dyani and Honovi. Paddling to steady her canoe, water sloshed up into her boat, soaking Moki. The turbulent rush spun her around backward, and then forward, and then sideways. Her strength intensified, somewhat, as she approached her home near the falls, but it wasn't enough to paddle against the unpredictable current.

At last, the twisters controlled by Heno and Chumana merged and collapsed into mist, and Honovi fell into the water beside Dyani. Dyani grabbed his father beneath his arms and buoyed him up several times in succession and at last, hauled him over the side of the canoe and into it. His eyes were closed at first, but Sallali pressed firmly with both her paws rapidly on his stomach in a bucket handle maneuver that sent spurts of water out of his mouth, spaying into the air like a fountain. His lungs sputtered. He coughed, and he rolled to the side, opened his eyes.

Lelewala's canoe had spun around again so that she faced them now. She shouted. "Dyani, shoot her!" The vicious undercurrents swirled her around again, and she looked back at her father and brother, as the flood washed her farther downstream. "You've got a shot. Shoot!"

Chumana smiled, overlooking all The Land. "Your brother will die in the flood, and you'll both be sucked into my whirlpool to drown in the Gorge."

"No," Dyani shouted.

Lelewala could not hold her canoe another moment in the current.

She and Moki were once again washed over Niagara Falls.

She jumped from the canoe and fell into Janok's arms below, on the rocks where he was waiting, watching the scene about the mist. She crashed into him, and they skidded onto a ledge of shale jutting into the basin of the falls. Moki plunked down onto Janok's head and bounced to shore, seconds later.

Dyani took aim at Chumana's heart and shot an arrow, praying as he released his redeeming shot.

He hit her.

The snake crashed into the river, creating a tortuous tsunami. Chumana smashed into the lower river. Her immense body blocked the flow of water. It directed its flow toward Heno's home, and washed out the Cave of the Winds, the entire palace. The tidal wave destroyed everything behind Niagara Falls in one swoop.

Ava, Ana, and Agatha floated out of the caves in a tug boat, screaming, as the aftershocks from Chumana's weight caused wave after wave that broadened each of them with a synergism unparalleled. They steered the boat toward Janok and Lelewala, where they bobbed about, gasping to keep their heads above water as they were pitched against cliffs of slate.

As Heno was washed down the river, he called, "Lelewala!"

Janok steered the bow of the tug boat about the base of Niagara Falls. It was thrown closer to the gushing water plummeting down beside them. Ava screamed.

She'd been tossed out of the boat.

Janok made a thunderous roar in his deepest voice yet. "Hang on! Ada, take the wheel."

He roared again, and his force created a rockslide, and the alluvium of the river drifted over the cliffs with each note of his thundering voice. The boulders that fell from the escarpment plunked below and settled, and they created a rock bridge that led beside the boat.

But Ada was still floundering in the rapids.

Janok extended his arms, leaning over the side of the tug boat, but a sudden wave washed the boat further from his sister. Finally, he jumped out of the boat and pulled her to the rock bridge. Lelewala jumped from the boat next, and Janok caught her. Ada and Agatha followed, into the water, then to the bridge. They ran across the rock bridge and climbed the stairs of the gorge, just before a wave smashed against the bridge, and the stairs, demolishing them.

Lelewala was shaking.

"I got you," said Janok, holding her.

Agatha said, "Our cave is destroyed."

Heno pushed back Chumana's dead body, her massive tail, as he had pushed back the rock, deepening the Niagara Gorge for millions of years before that day. His great force shook the earth. The Chief Annenraes and Dyani ran down the stone steps covered in lichens and moss, to the base of Niagara Falls.

Finally, the waters settled.

At this time, Heno parted the clouds, and the sky shone brightly on them. A golden ring of sunshine glowed around Lelewala. Her strength had fully returned, and she smiled and she stood beside Janok and she took his hand. Jaci fluttered down onto her shoulder.

Heno surveyed the damage, and his hands rose to the sky, and he said, "Chumana has destroyed our house, but not our home. I will bring a sun shower, a purging rain that will wash the poison from these waters."

Honovi knelt, and he bowed before Heno. "Thank you for saving my daughter, great God of Thunder. And Dyani, you have proven yourself a hero, and a skilled hunter. The snake maiden is dead, and your wedding curse is broken. Please forgive me, son. I beg you, return to the village. Our troubles are not over. There is still war between the Senecas, the Huron. A terrible famine. And the white man looms."

From the sumac, however, the white man was already near.

Perhaps, however, at this time, he was not such a threat, as they had perceived. Etienne Brulee and his men appeared, finally discovering Niagara Falls, as they had searched far and wide to find, and they stood before it in all its majesty where the sun came out. Dyani and Honovi and Lelewala and Heno and the sisters looked across the lower river to where they stood, and they smiled, and both sides made a sign of peace, at least for now.

Dyani said, "Of course, father."

Honovi also bowed before his son. "Please, son. If you'll return, I'll prepare a feast of venison, and the finest foods our tribe can spare. I'll clothe you in the robes of a chief, and you may serve beside me on the tribal council, soon to take my place."

Dyani took his father's hand, and he helped him to stand, and he hugged Honovi. "Father, yes. I would be honored."

Honovi was shocked, as he had prepared to hear the worst. "Wait, really?"

"Yes. Yes, of course, father." Dyani laughed, and he slapped his father on the back.

Looking into his son's eyes, Honovi said, "You are a wise hunter, son, and a loving brother. You will one day be a great chief."

Honovi and Dyani smiled. Beside them, Janok's sisters, Ava, Ada and Agatha, were ogling over Dyani.

Ava said, "I saw him first!"

"Yeah, but he's looking right at me." Agatha batted her eyelashes.

Ada said, "Wait, we never threw the bouquet." She grabbed a bunch of daisies from the riverbank, and she gave them to Lelewala, said, "Here Lele, toss this."

Lelewala turned, and she tossed the flowers over her right shoulder and she kissed Janok. The sisters pushed each other out of the way much like a bunch of lacrosse players, and they tackled each other, and Agatha landed on top of Ava with her legs askew in the air, and she caught the flowers. Her eyes went *ga-ga* then, as she fought her way up and she chased Dyani, who looked terrified of her, as though he'd just seen old Dry Fingers or the great White Bear again or other spirits of the dead.

As Agatha came running at Dyani, she jumped over a rock with her arms extended in a bear hug toward him, but he gasped and he ducked and Janok laughed.

"You'll have to excuse my sisters. Before now, we didn't get out of the Cave of the Winds much," said Janok.

Dyani exhaled, and he feigned a weak laugh, but then his eyes grew wide and surprised as Agatha sneaked up behind him and planted a kiss on his cheek and hugged him tightly as though she'd never let him go.

Heno was pleased. "Chumana is gone, but we'll need to move our home. Perhaps high above the clouds where Lelewala can see you, great Chief Honovi, and you, Dyani, too. Where her tears of joy will rain down, the mist on the great Niagara Falls." He turned to Lelewala. "That is—if you're still happy here, Lelewala."

Janok took Lelewala's hand. "Please, remain here, where you're alive and strong, my bride. I love you."

Lelewala's smile now was as bright as the sunshine itself. "Yes. Father, Janok and I are married. I love him." Then she turned and she kissed him and she turned back to her father, and she added, "I just feel terrible about running off."

Honovi said, "Do not worry, my daughter. As Heno said, you will live high in the clouds above the mist, and your breath will always be upon us. Remember, no river can return from its source, yet all rivers must have a beginning. Your story starts now."

Dyani pointed toward the sky, where a magnificent rainbow glowed. "Look, the rainbow." He asked, "Did you make it, Heno?"

"No, Dyani. It's a sign from He who is all things," said Heno.

"The Everything Maker," said Dyani.

Lelewala said, "Then I'll say goodbye for now, father, and go to my home."

She hugged her father, and Dyani. She held Janok's hand, and she, Heno and Ava and Ada, floated up then, fading into the mist.

Chief Honovi shed a tear, which dropped into the crystal waters, now serene, and before him, an image of Lelewala rose up, six years old, beside the table in their longhouse, boasting stories of folklore and myth and legend.

Birds soared above them. Dyani placed his arm around Agatha, but she began to float up into the mist along with her sisters, who waved down to him, smiling. He fell to the side, into the image that had now disappeared, and he stumbled a bit, into her spirit. Then, puzzled, he looked to the sky where Lelewala had gone now, and she, too, was above him, and she was looking down and she was smiling.

Sallali and Moki snuggled beside Dyani's feet. Shyly, Moki presented Sallali with a single daisy. Frekki waved, smiling, while Jaci fluttered up, high around the clouds where Lelewala was happy.

Agatha called down to them, "Dyani, don't forget about our date next week!"

The image faded from view where Lelewala and Janok kissed in the mist, a firm embrace, and the cirrus clouds gently covered Niagara Falls, and with it the only evidence left behind of this story, friends, so that it can only be passed on through the legends of those who tell it.

ABOUT THE AUTHOR

Melissa Franckowiak grew up visiting Niagara Falls every week, fascinated by the legends and history that surround this magnificent natural wonder. She is an MFA student at the University of Texas El Paso and writes for *Traffic East* magazine. Her short fiction piece, "The Very Pertinent News of Gabriel Vincent DeVil," placed in the 86th Annual Writer's Digest Literary Fiction Awards, and she has been published on MothersAlwaysWrite.com, Parent Co. and in *Nanny Magazine*.

Melissa set goals in early childhood to be a best-selling novelist and physician. She writes thrillers as Melissa Crickard. The daughter of an English and a science teacher, Melissa attended Georgia Institute of Technology and the University of Buffalo, and after being awarded two bachelor's degrees in physical therapy and chemistry, she advanced toward her MD degree from the State University of New York at Buffalo, going on to become a diplomat of the American Society of Anesthesiologists.

Melissa is the mother of two children, the owner of a chatty Panama Amazon parrot, and a lover of all things outdoors.

CPSIA information can be obtained
at www.ICGtesting.com
Printed in the USA
LVHW081348050422
715333LV00014B/732

9 781732 680814